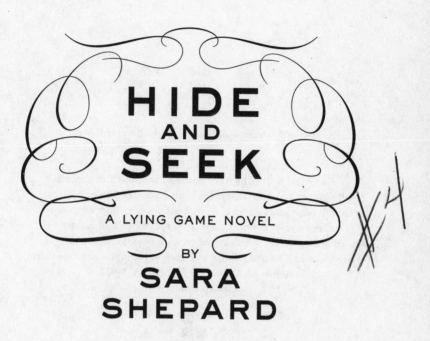

HIDE
AND
SEEK

A LYING GAME NOVEL

BY

SARA
SHEPARD

#4

HARPER TEEN
An Imprint of HarperCollinsPublishers

HarperTeen is an imprint of HarperCollins Publishers.

Hide and Seek

Produced by Alloy Entertainment
151 West 26th Street, New York, NY 10001

ISBN 978-0-06-186977-8 (pbk.)

Design by Liz Dresner

13 14 15 16 17   LP/RRDH   10 9 8 7 6 5 4 3 2 1
❖
First paperback edition, 2013

To Lanie

Cherish those who seek the truth
but beware of those who find it.

—VOLTAIRE

PROLOGUE

DEAD LIKE ME

I'd always thought the afterlife would be like an eternal stay at a resort on St. Barts—hot French waiters bringing me fruity drinks until the end of time, the azure Caribbean sky in a permanent sunset, a cool ocean breeze tickling my forever tanned skin. It would be my reward for living a full, fabulous, long life.

I couldn't have been more wrong.

Instead I died days before my eighteenth birthday and what was supposed to be an amazing senior year. And rather than sipping a mojito on a white-sand beach, I woke up in Las Vegas, tethered to a twin sister I never knew I had. I watched as Emma Paxton was forced into my life and had to begin impersonating me. I watched as she sat at my place at the table with my family and giggled with my friends, pretending she'd known them forever. I watched her read my journal, sleep in my bed, and try to figure out who killed me.

And I seemed to be stuck here until further notice. Everywhere Emma went, I went, too. Everything she knew, I knew as well—the problem was, I didn't know much beyond that. My life before I died was a question mark. Certain things have come back to me—like how I wasn't exactly the nicest girl at Hollier High, how I took for granted all the things I'd been given in life, and how I'd made plenty of enemies by playing vicious pranks on people who didn't deserve it. But everything else was a blank, including how I died, and who murdered me.

One thing I did know was that my killer was now watching Emma's every move right along with me, making sure that she plays along. I was a breath away when Emma found a note saying I was dead and warning her that if she didn't pretend to be me, she'd be dead, too. I felt the stars explode behind Emma's eyes when she was nearly strangled during a sleepover at my best friend Charlotte's house. I had a front-row seat when a light fixture in the school's auditorium careened toward her head. They were all warnings. My killer had been so close. And yet, neither of us had seen who it was.

It was up to my twin to catch my killer, and there was nothing I could do to help. It wasn't like I could communicate with her. Emma had cleared my best friends, Charlotte Chamberlain, Madeline Vega, and Gabby and Lili Fiorello, as murder suspects—they each had alibis for the night of my death. But the alibi she'd been counting on to clear my adoptive little sister, Laurel, suddenly wasn't so airtight.

Now I watched as my family sat on chaise lounges at the local country club, shading their eyes from the brutal Tucson sun. Emma settled into a seat next to Laurel and buried her nose in a magazine, but I could tell she was studying my sister as closely as I was.

Laurel pored over a leather-bound beverage menu through the shade of thick black Gucci sunglasses, then casually rubbed a dollop of tanning oil on her shoulders as though she didn't have a care in the world. Fury streaked through me. *I'll* never feel the sun on my skin again and it might be because of her. She had a motive, after all. We shared a secret crush—and I was the one who got Thayer in the end.

My mother pulled her BlackBerry from her straw Kate Spade beach tote. "You won't believe the way the RSVPs are pouring in for Saturday, Ted," she murmured, staring at the screen. "It looks like you'll be turning fifty-five with a bang."

"Mm-hmm," my dad said absently. It was unclear whether he really heard her. He was too busy looking across the pool at a tall, muscular boy running a hand through his dark hair.

Speak of the devil. Thayer Vega himself.

My heart thumped as Emma glanced in Thayer's direction. Laurel's gaze turned, too. No matter how cool my younger sister tried to play it, she couldn't hide the flash of hope that passed over her face. *Not on your life,* I thought angrily. I may be dead, but Thayer belongs to me—and *only* me. We'd had a secret relationship when I was alive, something that I'd only fully remembered a few days before. For a time, it had seemed like Thayer could have been my killer—we'd had a secret rendezvous the night I died. But thankfully, Emma had cleared him—someone had hit him with my Volvo, maybe aiming for me. Laurel had whisked Thayer off to the hospital, where he'd remained all night. I was relieved he wasn't the one who did it . . . until I realized that maybe the person who did was sitting next to Emma right now. Just because Laurel took Thayer to the hospital didn't mean she stayed with him. She could have come back to give me a piece of her mind . . . or to finish me off forever.

We all watched as Thayer climbed the metal steps of the diving board. He stalked to the end of the board, limping slightly, and tested the spring with a few bounces.

His stomach muscles rippled as he gathered momentum. He raised his tanned arms above his head and dived into the water, cutting the still surface with his perfect form. He stayed under for the length of the pool, little bubbles rising to the surface in his wake. I could almost feel the butterflies fluttering in my no-longer-there stomach as I watched him move beneath the water. Something about Thayer Vega still made me feel so *alive* and it took me a moment to realize that I wasn't.

Laurel's lips flattened into a grim line when Thayer surfaced and grinned at Emma, and I realized something else. If Emma's not careful, she'll end up just like me.

1

DON'T FEED THE EARTHLINGS

Emma Paxton leaned in close to the Saturn-shaped mirror in the Tucson Planetarium and pursed her lips as she reapplied a coat of cherry-flavored gloss. The entire dimly lit bathroom was astronomy-themed. The bathroom stalls were decorated with glow-in-the-dark star stickers, and the trash cans were in the shapes of rocket ships. A sign above the sink read WELCOME, EARTHLINGS. Two bobble-headed aliens stood on the G, their stubby fingers lifted in a wave.

Taking a deep breath, Emma stared at herself in the mirror. "This is your first official date with Ethan," she said to her reflection. She drew the last word out, savoring it. She couldn't remember the last time she'd been this excited about a guy—she'd dated guys before, but she moved around from foster home to foster home too often to ever really fall for someone. But lately, everything in her life had changed. A new home, a new family, and a new hot guy, Ethan Landry.

And a new identity, too, I wanted to add as I floated behind her, watching her in the mirror. As usual, my reflection wasn't anywhere to be seen. It had been that way ever since I popped into Emma's life when she was still living in Las Vegas. For all intents and purposes, Emma wasn't Emma anymore. She was me, Sutton Mercer. Other than my killer, Ethan was the only person who knew her true identity. He was even helping Emma figure out what happened to me.

Emma's phone pinged with a text. It was Ethan. HERE. JUST GOT TICKETS.

BE OUT IN A SECOND! she typed back.

Emma dried her hands, then pushed through the swinging door, fiddling with Sutton's locket. Her heart picked up speed when she spotted Ethan leaning against a curved, carpeted wall across the crowded room.

She loved how broad his shoulders looked in his gray polo and the way his hair fell into his dark blue eyes. His navy blue Chuck Taylors were unlaced, his hunter green T-shirt hugged his well-defined arms, and his jeans were perfectly broken in. She snaked around the line of people waiting to get into the planetarium and tapped him on the shoulder.

He turned around. "Oh, hey."

"Hey," Emma said, feeling suddenly shy. The last time she'd seen Ethan things had ended a little awkwardly. Thayer Vega had shown up at her house, and Emma hadn't introduced Ethan as her boyfriend. It had seemed cruel, somehow, to tell the boy who'd loved Sutton so desperately that she'd moved on. She'd called Ethan later to explain, and he'd seemed to understand. But what if he hadn't?

Before she had a chance to say anything, though, Ethan pulled Emma to him, and their lips met in a kiss. Emma sighed.

Lucky, I thought. What I wouldn't give to kiss someone again, although Thayer would be my top pick. I was happy for Emma, but I hoped all those love chemicals didn't distract her from the real task at hand: figuring out what the hell had happened to me.

"This looks fun," Emma said, lacing her fingers through his when they broke apart. "Thanks for bringing me here."

"Thanks for coming." Ethan pulled two tickets out of his back pocket. "It seemed appropriate for our first official date. It reminds me of how we first met," he said a little bashfully.

Emma blushed. This was *definitely* at least number three or four on the *Top Ten Cutest Ethan Moments* list. The night she'd arrived in Tucson, before he'd even figured out who she was, they'd looked up at the sky together, and Emma had told him how she named stars. Instead of making fun of her, Ethan had found it interesting.

Ethan walked toward the planetarium entrance. "Ready?" he asked as they stepped along a maroon-painted floor through heavy black curtains.

Emma smiled at him as they slipped into darkness. The air was cool and the room was silent. Through the glass ceiling above them, they could see the tiny blinking stars that dotted the night sky. For a moment she just stood there, getting lost in the complex patterns of the constellations. The sky was so vast and overwhelming, and for a few breaths at least, she was able to forget how complicated her own life had become. It didn't matter that she was playing someone else and putting her own life on hold. It didn't matter that her sister had been murdered and her latest suspect was Sutton's younger sister, Laurel, whom she'd thought was at Nisha Banerjee's sleepover the night of the crime, but had slipped away to take Thayer to the hospital after someone had hit him with Sutton's car. In comparison to the massive scope of the universe, nothing on earth really mattered.

"We still have a little while until the comet," Ethan

said, pressing a button on his diver's watch to illuminate the time. "Want to check out the exhibits in the other rooms?"

While New Age music played, Ethan and Emma stopped in front of an exhibit called *The Dirty Snowballs of Our Solar System*. It showed how comets form. Ethan coughed, then strutted up to a picture of a swirling comet and spoke in a high-pitched, nerdy voice. "So, you see, comets start out as chunks of rock and ice left over from the formation of stars and planets. And then the balls of rock get close to the sun, and the sun's heat melts some of the ice. How do you like that, missy?"

He hitched up his pants and rubbed his nose, and Emma suddenly realized he was impersonating Mr. Beardsley, their science teacher at Hollier. She burst out laughing. Mr. Beardsley was a zillion years old, forever talking in that nerdy voice, and calling all the girls "missy" and all the guys "son."

"You're good," she said, "but to really nail it, you have to lick your lips a bit more. And pick your nose."

Ethan made a face. "The idea of that guy picking his nose and then touching my test paper . . ."

"Horrifying." Emma shivered.

"I wish teachers made space more interesting," Ethan said, strolling to the next exhibit. His brow furrowed in concentration as he studied the photograph. His deep-set blue eyes glanced over the words written below it, his lips moving the tiniest bit as he read. "They make it so dry and bland, it's no wonder no one cares."

"I know what you mean," Emma said. "That's why I like *Star Trek: The Next Generation*. They make space so fantastical that you don't even realize when you're learning something."

Ethan's light eyes widened. "*You're* a Trekkie?"

"Guilty." Emma ducked her head, immediately cringing that she'd revealed something so dorky.

I quickly glanced around. Thank God no one *I* knew was in this place to overhear Emma's shameful admission. The last thing I needed to hit the gossip mill was that Sutton Mercer was into the ultimate nerd TV show.

Ethan just grinned. "Wow. You really *are* the perfect girl. I started a *Next Generation* fan club in seventh grade. I thought we could have marathon parties, dress up as our favorite characters, go to the convention, that sort of stuff. Shockingly no one joined."

Emma rolled her eyes. "I would have. I always had to watch the show alone. I couldn't tell you how many foster brothers and sisters made fun of me for it."

"Tell you what," Ethan said. "How about we have a Trekkie marathon party one of these days? I have DVDs of all the seasons."

"Deal," Emma answered, resting her head on his shoulder.

Ethan looked down at her. A slight flush passed over his face. "Any chance this Trekkie has a shot at taking you to the Harvest Dance?"

"I think that could be arranged," Emma said coyly. A headline flashed through her mind: *Foster Girl Gets Asked to Harvest Dance: Miracle!* She'd been making up diary headlines for her life ever since she could remember, and this was one for the front page.

There had been posters for the school's Harvest Dance up for a while now, touting the band they'd hired for the festivities, the float parade, and, of course, the Harvest Dance King and Queen. It was the kind of dance out of a movie, something Emma never thought she'd attend. Her mind played images of Ethan dressed in a dark suit, his arms around her waist as they slow-danced. She pictured the dress she'd wear from Sutton's closet, a short teal one that looked great against her pale skin and chestnut-brown hair. She'd feel like a princess.

I wanted to shake her. Didn't she know Sutton Mercer always got *new* dresses for dances?

A small child darted past Emma and pressed his hands against the glass in front of the comet display, breaking her from her reverie. She focused on the exhibit in front of them, a photograph of a black hole surrounded by a navy sky spotted with blazing stars. *A black hole is a region of space in which nothing, not even light, can escape*, read a placard next to the photo. Emma shivered, suddenly thinking of Sutton. Was this where she was now? Was this what the afterlife looked like?

Uh, not exactly, I thought.

"You okay?" Ethan asked, his brows knit in concern. "You just got really pale."

"Um, I need some air," Emma mumbled, feeling light-headed.

Ethan nodded and led her out the door marked EXIT and into a circular courtyard. Six stone paths were arranged like the spokes of a wheel. In the center was a massive, antique black telescope. Hedges opened up into a small alley, and across the road was a homey restaurant called Pedro's. Colorful Mexican pots sat in the windows, and chili-pepper lights were strung from the ceiling.

Emma and Ethan sat on a bench. She took several deep breaths as a wave of guilt crashed over her.

"Thinking about Sutton, aren't you?" Ethan asked, as if reading her mind.

Emma looked up at him. "Maybe I shouldn't be kissing boys and getting excited about going to dances when my sister's dead."

Ethan's fingers curled around hers. "But don't you

think she'd want you to be happy, too?"

Emma shut her eyes, hoping that was what Sutton wanted. But just thinking of Sutton reminded Emma she was in her own version of a black hole: Sutton's life. If she tried to escape being Sutton Mercer, she might die. Even if Sutton's killer was found, Emma would be exposed as a fraud—and then what would happen? She dreamed of the Mercer family taking her in and Sutton's friends welcoming her with open arms, but everyone might be furious that she duped them.

"*I* want to be with you," she said to Ethan after a long beat. "Not as Sutton. As *me*. I'm afraid that will never happen."

"Of course it will." Ethan cupped her chin in his hands. "All this will be over some day. Whatever happens, I'll be there for you."

Emma felt such a rush of gratitude that tears came to her eyes. She moved closer to Ethan, her hip pressing against his. She felt fluttery again as she gazed into his lake-blue eyes and smelled his woodsy aftershave. Ethan leaned in until his lips were a breath away from hers. She was about to kiss him when she heard a familiar laugh.

Emma's head snapped up. "Is that . . . ?" Two figures were being seated on Pedro's outdoor patio. One had blond hair and wore a pink sweater, and the other had on baggy pants and walked with a limp.

"Laurel and Thayer," Ethan whispered grimly, then made a face. "Well, there goes my idea for dinner afterward."

Laurel shook back her golden hair and slipped her arm through Thayer's. She did it casually, and for a moment, Emma wondered if Laurel didn't see her. But then Laurel's eyes cut across the street directly to Emma. A tiny hint of a smile appeared on her face. Not only did she know Emma was there, but she was squeezing Thayer's arm for Emma's benefit.

Bitch, I thought. Laurel had resented my secret relationship with Thayer for a long time. I'm sure she'd been waiting for this moment forever.

Thayer turned, too, and lifted his hand in a half-wave. Emma smiled back, but Ethan's hand tightened on Emma's protectively.

Emma turned to him. "Look, I know you don't like him," she said in a low voice. "But he's not dangerous. There's no way he could have killed Sutton. He was in the hospital all night, remember?"

Ethan looked like he had more to say on the topic, but he let out a sigh instead. "Yeah," he said grudgingly. "I guess. So where does that leave us? Is there anyone we suspect right now?"

Emma's gaze shifted to Laurel, who was peering at Emma over the menu. "Remember how I thought Laurel was at Nisha's the night Sutton disappeared?"

"Yeah, for the tennis team sleepover," Ethan said, nodding.

"Well she wasn't. At least not for the whole time."

Ethan's eyebrows shot up. "Are you sure?"

Emma drummed her fingertips on the bench's wrought-iron armrest. "Laurel is the one who picked Thayer up the night he was hit with the car. She's the one who drove him to the hospital. She couldn't be in two places at once. And if she lied about that . . ."

Ethan leaned forward, a light coming on in his eyes. "You think she dropped Thayer off at the hospital, then went back to the canyon to kill Sutton?"

"I hope not. But I can't rule her out if I don't know where she actually was. I need to find out if she went back to Nisha's or if she was out all night." She fidgeted with the hem of Sutton's black cotton miniskirt. "I've spent more time with Laurel than anyone else since I got to Tucson, but I don't completely understand her. One second, she's sweet. And the next, she acts like she wants to kill me."

"You've told me yourself that things between Sutton and Laurel seemed . . . strained."

Emma nodded. "I know. Mrs. Mercer talked to me about it last week. She said Laurel's always been jealous of me—I mean, of Sutton." Emma shook her head slightly. The longer she play-acted her sister, the fuzzier the line became where Sutton ended and she began.

Ethan glanced across to Pedro's, where Laurel and Thayer were sharing a basket of tortilla chips. "Maybe. But from the outside, at least, it seemed like Sutton might have been jealous of Laurel, too. After all, Laurel is the Mercers' biological daughter. It always seemed like being adopted made Sutton feel a little . . . *lost*. I saw her in the library at school once poring over a book on genealogy. The look on her face . . ." Ethan hesitated. "Well, I'd never seen Sutton Mercer look sad before."

A swell of vulnerability hit me like wave. I had no memory of that, but ever since I'd woken up at Emma's place in Las Vegas, I'd felt a deep, familiar ache that had nothing to do with being dead. I'd always known I was adopted, and my parents had told me over and over that I was special because they'd chosen me to be their daughter. But the thought that my real mom hadn't wanted me made me feel adrift and empty, like a piece of me was permanently missing.

But how had Ethan, whom I'd barely known, seen through me like that? Was I more transparent than I thought?

"I guess Laurel had what Sutton never could—a

biological family," Emma said softly, knowing exactly how her twin felt. When she was five years old, her and Sutton's birth mother, Becky, had left her at a friend's house . . . and never come back.

Emma sighed deeply. "Laurel just seems so angry. She was able to keep a lid on it until Thayer showed up in Sutton's room and Mr. Mercer called the cops on him. But now that he's back, it feels like she'd do anything to keep him away from the girl he thinks is Sutton—the girl Laurel knows he loves."

"What's the saying? That people kill for money, love, or revenge?" Ethan asked, rubbing his hands together as a cool breeze blew through the courtyard. "Maybe she wanted to get rid of the competition."

"Well, she certainly accomplished that. It looks like they're on a date." Emma glanced across the courtyard again. Thayer rested a hand on Laurel's shoulder. She fed him a chip loaded with guacamole, then shot another self-satisfied smirk in Emma's direction. Emma wondered what happened to Caleb, Laurel's boyfriend as of yesterday. Laurel probably didn't even remember his name.

I followed Emma's gaze back over to my little sister. Thayer was now giving his order to the waitress, his posture easy and natural. Laurel watched him adoringly, hugging the pale pink sweater-wrap that engulfed her tiny frame. I narrowed my eyes. I recognized that sweater. It, like Thayer, was mine.

Maybe my mom and Ethan were right—maybe Laurel wanted everything that was mine. And maybe, just maybe, she had killed me to get it all.

2

TO GRANDMOTHER'S HOUSE WE GO

The following evening, Emma turned into the Mercers' neighborhood, groaning as her feet pushed the pedal.

"The *pain*," she grumbled. They'd just had the worst tennis practice ever—it had involved a five-mile run *before* a grueling scrimmage and drills—and she could barely move her legs. Why couldn't Sutton have just been a couch potato?

Laurel sat in the passenger seat, scrolling through her iPhone and ignoring Emma's comment, even though she had to be in agony, too.

"So did you have a nice date with Thayer last night?" Emma couldn't help but ask.

Laurel looked up and gave her a saccharine smile. "Yes, as a matter of fact. It was *really* romantic—I think we might even go to the Harvest Dance together."

"What about Caleb?"

Laurel blinked, caught off guard. "Caleb and I never were exclusive," she said after a moment.

Emma sniffed. *It certainly looked that way at the Homecoming Dance,* she wanted to say.

"Why do you care, anyway?" Laurel snapped, turning back to her phone. "Now that you have Ethan?"

Emma flinched at the disgusted way Laurel said Ethan's name. Sutton's friends had seemed pretty accepting of him, Laurel especially. She'd been the one who'd encouraged her to come clean with their friends about their romance. But was that an act? Or, if Laurel *had* killed Sutton, was it a secret wink-wink, nudge-nudge as if to say, *I know you're not my real sister. I know you never cared about Thayer.*

"No, I don't care," Emma said tightly. "I was just making conversation."

But *I* cared. What if Thayer *did* like my sister? Would he do that to me? Then again, he probably figured I'd abandoned him for Ethan. If only he knew the truth.

Emma turned up the Mercers' driveway. The sun was setting behind their two-story adobe home, a home Emma had gawked at when she'd first laid eyes on it. She still had trouble accepting that she actually lived here. The orange rays glinted off Mr. Mercer's Range Rover. Next to it was a gleaming black Cadillac Emma had never seen before. Its California license plate said FOXY 70.

"Whose car is that?" Emma asked, turning off the ignition.

Laurel gave her a funny look. "Uh, Grandma's?" she said in a *duh* voice.

Heat rose to Emma's cheeks. "Oh, right. I knew that. She just hasn't been here in a while." She was used to covering for her I'm-not-Sutton gaffes by now, not that she felt any more graceful about it. And, of course, Grandma Mercer would be yet another person Emma had to fool into believing she was Sutton.

Laurel was already climbing out of the car. "Sweet," she said, tossing a lock of honey-blond hair over her shoulder. "Dad's grilling." And with that, she slammed the door.

Emma pulled up the parking brake. She'd forgotten Mr. Mercer's mom was flying in for his fifty-fifth birthday party, which Mrs. Mercer had been frantically planning for the past few weeks. So far, she'd arranged the caterers, organized a band, pored over the guest list, micromanaged the seating arrangements, and dealt with dozens of other details. Grandma was here to help, too.

With a deep, fortifying breath, Emma climbed out and lifted her tennis bag from the trunk. She followed Laurel along a stone path that led to the Mercers' backyard. A woman's gravelly, throaty laugh cut through the air, and as soon as Emma turned the corner, she saw Mr. Mercer standing at the grill, holding a tray of skewered veggies. Next to him was a well-preserved older woman holding a martini. She was pretty much what Emma pictured when she imagined a Grandma Mercer: poised, classy, elegant.

The woman's face broke into a cool smile when she saw the girls. "Darlings."

"Hey, Grandma!" Laurel called out.

The old woman moved toward them, amazingly not spilling a single drop of alcohol onto the stone patio. She looked Laurel up and down. "Gorgeous, as usual." Then, she turned to Emma and gave her a big hug. Her pearl necklace jabbed into Emma's collarbone, and she felt surprisingly solid for such a petite woman.

Emma returned the hug, inhaling the woman's gardenia perfume. When Sutton's grandmother pulled away, she held Emma at arm's length and examined her closely. "My goodness," she said, shaking her head. "I've obviously been gone too long. You look so . . . *different*."

Emma tried not to squirm in the woman's grip. *Different* wasn't exactly the look she was going for.

Sutton's grandmother squinted. "Is it your hair?" She put a bony, perfectly manicured finger to her lips. "What's with the bangs in your eyes? How can you *see*?"

"It's the way everyone's wearing them these days," Emma said, pushing her bangs out of her eyes. She'd let them grow a little because Sutton's bangs were this long, too, but deep down, she agreed with Sutton's grand-mother.

Grandma wrinkled her nose, not satisfied. "You and I need to have a little talk," she said sharply. "I hear you're still giving your parents trouble?"

"Trouble?" Emma squeaked.

Grandma's mouth became a straight line. "Something about shoplifting from a boutique not so long ago."

Emma's throat went dry. It was true that she'd stolen a purse from a boutique to gain access to Sutton's police file—Quinlan, a detective on the force, had a huge folder on Sutton full of various Lying Game pranks she'd played throughout the years.

As Grandma stared unwaveringly at Emma, a memory zoomed back to me: I was sitting in my bedroom about to upload tennis team pictures to Facebook when I heard voices in the living room. Camera in hand, I tiptoed to the staircase, straining to hear. It sounded like Grandma and my dad were arguing, but about *what*? And that's when my brand-new digital camera slipped from my hand and landed on the top step with a thud. "Sutton?" my dad said. He and my grandmother moved from the living room to the base of the stairs before I could scamper off.

They stared at me in the same way Grandma was looking at Emma right now.

"We've moved past that," Mr. Mercer said, flipping steaks on the grill. He was wearing a black apron with a coiled rattlesnake on the front, and his graying hair was combed off his forehead. "She's been doing really well lately, actually. Got the highest grade on a German test recently. She's getting good grades in English and history as well."

"You're too easy on her," Grandma snapped. "Was she even punished for what she did?"

Mr. Mercer seemed to wilt a little. "Well, yes. She was grounded."

Grandma guffawed. "For what? A *day*?"

Actually, Mr. Mercer *had* lifted the grounding early. Everyone shut their mouths awkwardly, and for a few long beats, the only sounds were the sizzling grill and the calling birds. Emma glanced at Grandma Mercer, who was staring at her son. It was strange to see someone boss Mr. Mercer around.

After a beat, Mr. Mercer cleared his throat. "So, girls. Chicken or steak?"

"Chicken, please," Emma said, eager to change the subject. She took a seat next to Laurel on one of the green patio chairs assembled around a glass outdoor table. The patio door creaked open, and out bounded Drake, the Mercers' enormous Great Dane. As usual, he made a beeline straight for Emma—it was like he sensed she was uncomfortable with dogs and was trying his hardest to make her like him. Tentatively she stuck out her hand and let him lick it. She'd been afraid of dogs ever since a Chow bit her, but she was slowly getting used to the massive animal.

Mrs. Mercer emerged from the house next, a blue-and-white-checkered tablecloth in one hand and her BlackBerry, which was always ringing, in the other. Her expression was drawn, but when she saw her daughters sitting at the table, she broke into a smile. Even when Mrs. Mercer was stressed, the sight of Emma and Laurel seemed to lift her mood. It was a new experience for Emma. Usually parent-types looked at her with a tight-lipped, where's-my-paycheck expression.

"So, girls. How was practice?" Mrs. Mercer raised the checkered cloth in the air and let it settle over the glass table.

"Murder." Laurel grabbed a carrot stick from a vegetable platter on the grill and crunched down on it loudly.

Emma flinched at Laurel's choice of word, but forced a tired smile on her face. "We had a five-mile run," she explained.

"In addition to tennis drills?" Mrs. Mercer squeezed Emma's shoulder. "You must be exhausted."

Emma nodded. "I'll definitely need a hot shower tonight."

"I need one, too," Laurel said petulantly. "Don't take one of your thirty-minute soaks."

Emma opened her mouth, about to tell Laurel she'd never take a thirty-minute soak, but then she realized that was probably something Sutton did. She'd started another list as well: *Ways I'm Not Sutton*. It helped her remember who *she* was amidst all this. When she'd come to Tucson, all she'd brought was a small duffel, which had been stolen when she arrived. The rest of her belongings—her guitar, her savings, and the secondhand laptop she'd gotten at a pawn shop—were stashed in a locker at the Vegas bus station. Lately, it felt like she'd left her identity in that locker, too. The only person she kept in contact with from her old life was her best friend, Alex Stokes, who she'd barely spoken to since she got to Tucson. Alex thought Emma was living happily with Sutton at the Mercers'. Emma couldn't tell her the truth, and all the lies made the distance between them feel too great to cross.

Mr. Mercer swooped up to the table and set down five plates full of grilled food. "Chicken for my girls, steak for me and Grandma—medium rare—and super-well-done for my beautiful wife." He pushed a lock of hair out of Mrs. Mercer's eyes and gave her a kiss on the cheek.

Emma smiled. It was nice to see that two people could

be together for decades and still be so solid. Rarely did she ever live with a foster family who had two parents who lived together, let alone loved each other.

It was something I noticed now that I was dead, too—my parents *did* really care for each other. They finished each other's sentences. They were still affectionate and sweet to one another. It was never something I'd appreciated when I was alive.

Grandma Mercer turned her steely blue eyes on Mr. Mercer. "You look thin, dear. Are you eating enough?"

Mr. Mercer chuckled. "Seriously? My washboard abs are no more."

"He eats *plenty*. Trust me," Mrs. Mercer said. "You should see our grocery bills." Then her BlackBerry chimed, and she glanced at the screen and frowned. "I don't believe it. The party is on *Saturday*, and now the florist tells me she can't do desert globemallows in the table bouquets. I really wanted to keep all the flowers and plants native to Arizona, but I may have to do a few bouquets of calla lilies if the florist can't get her act together."

Emma laughed good-naturedly. "Tragic, Mom!"

Sutton's grandmother's clear blue eyes narrowed, her face suddenly hard. "Attitude," she warned. Her voice was so sharp it could cut glass.

Emma's cheeks burned. "I was just kidding," she said in a tiny voice.

"I highly doubt that," Grandma said, spearing her steak.

Yet again, there was a long, awkward silence. Mr. Mercer dabbed at his mouth with his napkin, and Mrs. Mercer fiddled with the Chanel bangle around her wrist. Emma wondered what subtext she was missing here.

I racked my foggy memory for an answer, but I couldn't come up with anything. Grandma definitely had it in for me, though.

Mrs. Mercer looked around the table, then shut her eyes. "I forgot the pitcher of water and the glasses. Girls, can you go inside and get them?" She sounded weary, as though Grandma had drained her of strength.

"Sure," Laurel said brightly. Emma rose, too, eager to get away from Grandma. They made their way into the Spanish-tiled kitchen. The dark soapstone countertops gleamed, and pineapple-themed dish towels hung neatly from the oven handle. Emma was just grabbing the water pitcher when she felt a hand on her shoulder.

"Sutton," Mr. Mercer said in a hushed voice. "Laurel."

Laurel froze with a tray of ice-filled glasses in her hand.

"I heard Thayer is coming back to school tomorrow," Mr. Mercer said, shutting the patio door. The sound of Grandma critiquing Mrs. Mercer's choice of salsa music for the party instantly evaporated. "Just because he's out of jail doesn't change anything. I want you two to keep your distance."

Laurel set her mouth in a line. "But Dad, he's my best friend. You didn't have a problem with him before."

Mr. Mercer's eyebrows shot up. "That was before he broke into our house, Laurel. People change."

Laurel lowered her head and shrugged. She didn't, Emma noticed, make any mention of going on a date with Thayer yesterday.

"Sutton?" Mr. Mercer stared at Emma next.

"Um, I'll stay away," Emma mumbled.

"I mean it, girls," Mr. Mercer said sternly. He stared straight at Emma when he spoke, and once again, Emma wondered what subtext she was missing. "If I find out that you're hanging out with him, there will be consequences."

And then he turned on his heel and marched back to the patio.

As soon as he shut the door, Laurel faced Emma. There was a sickly smile on her face. "That was smart to not mention seeing us last night," she said icily.

Emma made a face. "If Thayer means that much to you, *you* should have said something. Convinced Dad not to worry."

Laurel flicked her blond hair off her shoulder and stepped closer. Her breath smelled like spicy barbecue sauce. "We all know Dad can be overprotective. If you know what's good for you, you'll keep your mouth shut. Got it?"

Emma nodded faintly. After Laurel turned toward the patio, Emma crumpled against the island, suddenly exhausted. *If you know what's good for you.* Was that . . . a *threat*?

I didn't know either. And I wasn't eager to find out.

3

VOLLEYING WITH THE ENEMY

By the time the Mercers finished dinner, the sun had set, the frogs had started croaking, and there was a chill to the air. Emma had a pile of German homework, but being in the same house as Laurel without being able to make any headway on the investigation filled her with restless adrenaline. Though she was still aching from practice, she found herself slipping on gray leggings and taking off for the tennis courts down the block. She didn't plan on hitting the ball very hard.

The courts were empty. Only a few people were out walking their dogs on the trails, and a couple was talking quietly by a Mini Cooper in the parking lot. Emma selected the far court, which had a solid wall for solo play, and dropped three quarters into the meter that turned on the overhead lights. A *pop* sounded as she pried open a new container of fuzzy yellow balls. She bounced one on her racket a few times before lobbing it gently into the wall, the previous aches and pains from the grueling practice melting away.

It felt good to hit the ball over and over, losing herself in her thoughts. *Could* Laurel have killed Sutton? Emma didn't have any proof, but she also didn't have proof that Laurel *didn't* do it, either. If only she could find something personal of Laurel's, like a diary—or her cell phone. Laurel guarded the thing with her life, but maybe there was a way to get her hands on it.

Of course there was one other way to figure out if Laurel had an alibi for that night: asking Thayer if she'd stayed with him at the hospital. The idea of talking with Thayer was nerve-racking. Emma had fooled everyone except Ethan into thinking she was Sutton, but Thayer and Sutton had major history; they'd been in love. But the same reason that made it scary made it intriguing—Emma was so curious about Sutton, and Thayer knew her better than anyone.

I'd give anything to see Thayer as much as possible, even if I couldn't touch him. On the other hand, if Thayer didn't realize Emma wasn't me after spending time with her, well, I wasn't sure I could deal with that.

Suddenly, the overhead lights snapped off, leaving Emma in darkness. She bent over her legs, breathing hard, letting the ball bounce off the wall and roll to the other end of the court. Footsteps rustled in the grass beside the court, and she stood up, tensed.

"Hello?" Emma called. "Ethan?" The tennis courts had been Emma and Ethan's meeting place since her arrival in Tucson, though they hadn't planned to get together that night.

There was no answer, but she heard rustling sounds in the underbrush surrounding the courts. Her eyes not yet adjusted to the darkness, Emma inched closer to the backboard and felt her way along the smooth wood. The toe of her sneaker touched the chain-link fence, making a *clink* sound. She froze, knowing she'd just given away her position. A second later, the electricity powered back on, flooding the court with light and illuminating a figure standing at the edge of the court.

Emma screamed.

The figure whipped around and screamed, too. But then Emma saw who it was: Nisha Banerjee, Sutton's rival and tennis cocaptain. Emma collapsed against the fence, pressing her hands to her eyes. "Nisha! You scared the shit out of me!"

"You were the one lurking on the court in the dark!" Nisha cried. For a moment, she looked furious, but then she dissolved into giggles. "God. We both screamed like six-year-olds who just saw their first horror movie."

"I know." Emma breathed out, willing her heart to slow down. "We're pathetic, huh?"

Nisha took a few steps toward her. She was wearing a red Adidas tennis dress and matching wrist sweatbands. Her pristine sneakers were tied with tiny bows and her black hair was tucked behind a violet-colored headband. But even though she looked perfect, her eyes were glassy, and her fingers trembled ever so slightly. Nisha was not someone who liked being even the slightest bit out of control.

"You playing solo?" Nisha asked.

Emma nodded.

"Oh. I was going to do that, too," Nisha said. She ducked her head and tucked her racket under her arm. "I'll leave you to it, then."

But then she gave Emma a long glance. Her brown eyes looked tired, and there were sloping circles beneath them. Emma softened. She was so used to sparring with Nisha, but right now, the girl looked weary and a little bit shy.

She looked different to me, too. It was strange seeing people from such a removed perspective, like everything I'd once thought to be true about them was nothing more than a carefully constructed facade.

Emma cleared her throat. "Why aren't you playing at the courts closer to your house?" Nisha lived near Sabino

Canyon, and Emma had seen a court at the entrance to her neighborhood.

Nisha shrugged. "It was crowded. And I felt like being alone."

Emma spun her racket in her hand. "Well, since we're both here, do you want to volley?"

Nisha's jaw twitched. Emma could tell by the tiny flutter of her eyelashes that Nisha had wanted her to ask exactly that. "Um, sure," she said, playing it cool. "If you want."

"I do," Emma said, realizing it was true. She had never seen the girl look vulnerable, and something about it struck a chord. But there was something else she'd thought of, too: Nisha had been Laurel's alibi on August thirty-first, the night Sutton went missing. She'd told Emma that Laurel had been at her house the whole night, when Laurel definitely hadn't. Had Nisha lied? Or had Laurel snuck out after Nisha had fallen asleep?

They strolled to opposite sides of the court. Nisha adjusted her tennis skirt, and Emma snickered. "I have to say. Only you would dress like Serena Williams on a dark and abandoned court, Nisha," she teased, tossing the ball high in the air and whacking it hard.

"I'll take that as a compliment," Nisha said as the ball whizzed toward her. She slammed the ball hard. Emma lunged for it, but it flew past her, clanking against the chain-link fence.

"Fair enough." Emma laughed. "Love-fifteen," she said, trotting over to retrieve the ball. This time she hit a mild shot over the net, which Nisha easily returned, setting the tone for a friendly volley.

They played a few rounds, both of them remarking how amazing it was that they still had energy after today's grueling practice. After Emma hit a backhand into the net, Nisha took a break to drink from her water bottle. "I hear you're dating Ethan Landry."

"That's right," Emma said, blushing a little.

Nisha wiped her mouth. "So he actually *talks*, then?"

"Sure he talks. A lot."

"That's news to me." Nisha placed her water bottle on the bench. "My mom used to call him Silent E. We took the same bus, and he never said one word to me—or anyone—the entire eighth-grade school year."

"He's just shy," Emma mumbled, having forgotten that Nisha and Ethan were neighbors. It hurt to hear about Ethan's quiet days. She hated that he hadn't had many friends.

"Well, shy's cool." Nisha swung her legs, then gave Emma a jealous glance. "And he's certainly gorgeous."

That was more like it. "I know," Emma said, shivering with pleasure, thinking about the kisses she'd shared with Ethan at the planetarium last night. "What's going on with you and Garrett?" Nisha had shown up with Sutton's ex at the Homecoming Dance a few weeks ago, looking very pleased with herself.

Nisha shrugged. "Nothing really." Then she took another sip of water and changed the subject. "Remember when we were little, and we used to count how many shots we could get back and forth before one of us messed up?" she asked. "Our own *world records*," she went on, deepening her voice to sound like a sports announcer.

Emma smiled to herself. For as many items she'd put on the *Ways I'm Not Sutton* list, there were so many quirky things they did that were just the same. She'd counted volleys with her Russian foster brother, Stephan, when they'd played endless rounds of ping-pong in the basement. Even now she often found herself counting in practice and matches out of habit.

"That feels like an eternity ago," Nisha went on. "I always liked it when you and Laurel included me." Then her lips tightened, like she'd said too much. She took a hard pull from the water bottle. "Anyway," she said toughly. "Ready for me to whip your ass some more?"

But Emma didn't move. "It's lonely to be an only child," she said softly.

Nisha looked at her sharply. "It's not like you'd know. You have Laurel."

Emma bit her lip and looked away. She'd been talking about herself, of course—even with all of her foster brothers and sisters, she still felt adrift and alone. She'd longed for a brother or a sister—family of *some* kind. It was one of those moments where she wanted to tell Nisha about *her* experience, but couldn't.

Then Nisha sighed. "But you're right, it is lonely. Especially now that my mom is . . . gone. I love my dad, but he's not exactly great company."

Emma nodded. She knew that Nisha's mom had died over the summer, but Nisha had never once mentioned it. Right now, though, it seemed like she *wanted* to talk about it. Like she wanted someone to listen.

"You guys were really close, huh?" Emma asked.

A cloud passed over the moon. A roadrunner darted across the parking lot. Nisha traced the Nike logo on her water bottle. "We loved to cook together and make these massive Indian feasts. My mom thought I was too thin. She was always trying to fatten me up."

"That seems to be a mom thing," Emma said, thinking of Grandma Mercer and her son. "Do you still . . . talk to her?"

Nisha gave Emma a strange look, her face reddening. "How did you know?"

Emma stared at the white net in the middle of the court. "It was just a guess. I talk to my birth mom."

Nisha raised an eyebrow. "But you've never even *met* your birth mom."

"I know," Emma said quickly. "But I know she's out there. And I wonder about her all the time. When things get really hard, I talk to her. She always listens." She smiled wryly. Imaginary Becky was much more attentive than real Becky had ever been.

Nisha rolled the tennis ball under her palm. "I talk to her while I'm in the car," she said quietly. "Talking to her in my house seems risky—I don't want my dad to hear. But when I'm driving to school or wherever, I have whole monologues with her. When I pause at stoplights, still talking to myself, I can see people looking. They probably just assume I'm on a Bluetooth or something, not talking to my dead mother."

Suddenly, she drew back and stared at Emma as though she'd forgotten Emma was there. "You probably think that's super-freaky, huh? Are you going to tell your friends about this?" she asked, blinking rapidly.

"I won't!" Emma placed her hand over her heart. "I swear. Your secret is safe with me." When Nisha still looked worried, she lightly touched the girl's shoulder. "I'm glad you told me. I think it's great you talk to her. Honestly? It would be weird if you didn't."

Nisha fiddled with the sweatband around her wrist, still looking embarrassed. "Well, I should get going. That English term paper is calling my name."

"Yeah, I have about ten minutes before my dad calls

the police. He's been running a tight ship these days."
Emma packed up her bag. As the two girls walked off
the court toward the street, matching each other step-for-
step, Emma realized she'd forgotten all about asking Nisha
where Laurel really was the night Sutton died. Instead,
she'd been too busy bonding with Sutton's sworn enemy.
And it had been kind of . . . *nice.*

I was all for it, as long as Emma kept her head. Nisha
had always been a thorn in my side, and I didn't see her
changing now. Still, you know what they say: Keep your
friends close, and your enemies closer. Especially when
that enemy might know the truth about where Emma's
number-one murder suspect was the night I died.

4

THE UNGIVING TREE

On Tuesday morning, Emma pulled into the lot of Hollier High, which was set in the hills of Tucson. Hundreds of cacti, some spiny, some flowering, served as the landscape. The mountains rose up behind the school, red and majestic. The lot was bustling with students. A Jeep full of jocks drove past, an old Dave Matthews song blaring over the speakers. A group of pretty girls in matching leather jackets swapped lip glosses next to a vintage convertible. School buses huffed around the corner, the track team did a final loop around the field for their morning practice, and a bunch of kids were huddled near the spiny shrubs, trying to hide that they were smoking.

As Emma got out of the car, two girls in miniskirts walked by, gossiping loudly about Thayer. Today was his first day back at school. Rumors about his absence had been swirling for weeks: that he'd spent time in jail, that he'd been working on a major Hollywood movie, that he'd had a sex change. Only the first was true: He'd been in jail for a couple days the other week for trespassing on the Mercers' property and resisting arrest.

Emma heard a door slam next to her. Sutton's two closest friends, Madeline and Charlotte, emerged from a black SUV. Madeline, who had sleek, black hair and a heart-shaped face, was in high-heeled boots, and her slim-cut jeans seemed like they were made specifically for her dancer's body. The inside of her wrist was tattooed with a single red rose bud, and on the back of her iPhone was a sticker that said SWAN LAKE MAFIA. Emma still wasn't exactly sure what that meant. Charlotte, who was slightly pudgy but had beautiful, creamy skin and thick, red hair, slung an enormous monogrammed Louis Vuitton bag over her shoulder just as a white SUV pulled into the space next to them. The Twitter Twins, Lilianna and Gabriella, whose only matching features were their blond hair and blue eyes, tumbled out. *All of the Lying Game is present and accounted for*, Emma thought, thinking about Sutton's pranking clique. Well, *almost* all of the Lying Game—Laurel had evaded Emma's offer to take her to school today, saying she had "made other arrangements."

Lili clicked over to Emma on her black stilettos. "The administration should just reserve these parking spots for us permanently," she trilled, placing a hand on her punkish chain-link necklace. Lili and Gabby had only become official members of the Lying Game a few weeks ago, and they brought up their newfound status as often as possible.

"I can just see it now," Gabby jumped in. "'Reserved for Gabby.' That would look awesome on a sign." She pushed a lock of straight blond hair behind her ear. She was Lili's opposite, wearing a pale pink cashmere shrug, a preppy green polo, skinny jeans, and patent-leather flats with bows on the toes. She looked ready to go to a croquet match.

Madeline's phone beeped in her cavernous suede bag. She smiled when she pulled it out. "My brother is such a dork," she said, rolling her eyes happily. Her fingers flew across the keyboard as she crafted a response.

"Where *is* Thayer?" Gabby looked around, like he might be hiding behind Madeline's SUV.

"He's coming in a bit later," Madeline said. "The principal didn't want him to create a stir before school. He just texted me that he's hanging out in his room, bored out of his mind, playing Mario Kart." She snickered. "He hasn't played that since he was about nine."

The first bell rang in the distance, signaling that they had ten minutes before classes started. "Is Laurel with him?" Emma blurted. She hadn't meant to say it, but where else could Laurel be? She'd disappeared this morning with no explanation.

Madeline looked up sharply. "I don't think so."

"Are you sure?" Emma pressed.

"Why do you care?" Charlotte nudged Emma's side. "I thought you had a new hottie, Sutton."

"I do," Emma insisted. "I was just—"

"I wish you would stay away from Thayer," Madeline interrupted. "I love you, Sutton, but you messed him up big time. I can't have him running off again."

"I don't want to *be* with Thayer!" Emma protested through her teeth. "I was just wondering where Laurel was."

I couldn't help but glare at Madeline. I hadn't messed Thayer up. If anything, Thayer had messed *me* up, running off without telling me where he was going, then sneaking back into town to meet me in secluded places like Sabino Canyon. His limp might have been because of me, but *I* wasn't the one who caused it.

"Okay, this convo is officially boring me." Charlotte tossed her red hair over her shoulder. "C'mon, guys. I'm dying for coffee. I barely got any sleep last night. My parents kept me up all night with one of their marathon shout-fests."

"Lattes on me," Lili said, adjusting the headband in her hair.

Charlotte and the Twitter Twins headed toward the school's coffee kiosk. Emma followed, and Madeline fell in step next to her, which Emma figured was an olive branch. She tried not to take it personally that Madeline had basically barred her from speaking to her brother. She was just being protective of him.

They pushed onto the front lawn and took a sharp left, dodging kids carrying instrument cases, a girl with her nose stuck in a book, and a couple making out next to the water fountain. The announcement board was plastered with posters for the Harvest Dance, most of them featuring a white-silhouetted couple dancing together. When they reached the front entrance, they noticed a crowd gathered just outside the doors. Emma's first thought was that Thayer had returned early, but then Charlotte stopped short in front of her so quickly that she almost bumped into her back.

"Holy shit," Gabby breathed.

Madeline pushed her tortoiseshell sunglasses to the top of her head. "What the hell?"

A row of mesquite trees stood sentinel in front of the school. Silver streamers were twined through the spindly branches and dozens of lacy bras and blown-up condoms hung from the limbs. Penis balloons bobbled around a trunk, which had been spray-painted black. Strung across the trees was a sign that read BOW DOWN AND WORSHIP US, BITCHES. The whole effect was that of a naughty Christmas tree—or a Vegas bachelorette party gone awry.

"Oh my God," Clara Hewlitt, a dark-haired sophomore from the tennis team, breathed, her brown eyes wide.

"It has to be them," whispered a lanky junior with a ratty blond ponytail.

All eyes clapped on Emma and Sutton's friends. Emma looked around the courtyard, seeing a lot of faces she recognized, but a lot she still didn't. Sutton's ex, Garrett Austin, was standing next to his younger sister, Louisa, glaring at Emma with disdain. Lori, a girl from her pottery class, was looking at Emma with awe and respect. Nisha's cherry-colored lips were pursed as she read over the graffiti. Emma caught her eye but Nisha looked away.

Lili whipped around and looked at Emma, Madeline, and Charlotte. Her face was pinched with hurt. "Did you guys leave us out of a prank?"

Charlotte shook her head slowly. "This wasn't us."

"Honest," Madeline added quickly. "Not unless I did this while sleepwalking."

"Oh." Lili brightened. "Well, in that case . . ." She and Gabby yanked out their iPhones and held it up to the mayhem. "Everyone say *Twitpic*!"

Madeline grabbed the phone from Lili's hand before

Lili could snap the photo. "This isn't *cool*. It's just lame vandalism."

Lili clapped her mouth closed, looking cowed. "Who do you think did it?"

Madeline scanned the crowd. Suddenly her eyes widened. "Over there," she hissed, nodding at something near the lamppost.

Emma followed her gaze. A group of four girls stood in a huddle, their backs to the defaced trees. They all had on dark skinny jeans and Converse sneakers and sported edgy haircuts. Judging by the tough, bossy look on the face of a blond girl with dip-dyed ends, Emma guessed she was the leader. Emma could detect an air of satisfaction from each and every one of them.

"No *way*," Charlotte whispered.

"I'm almost positive," Madeline murmured. "It has to be them."

Gabby used her phone to zoom in on the girls' faces. Dip-dyed Girl looked even meaner and tougher in close-up. "*Bitches.*"

"Who are they?" Emma asked, not caring if Sutton was supposed to already know.

I didn't, though. They looked young, likely freshmen, meaning I never would have met them. I'd died before the first day of school, and I wouldn't have been caught dead fraternizing with kids from junior high.

"Ariane Richards, Coco Tremont, Bethany Ramirez, and Joanna Chen," Madeline said. "This sophomore in my dance class told me about them. They were the *us* of Saguaro Middle School. But their pranks were super-lame. Stealing the school mascot, writing nasty things about girls in lipstick across their lockers, replacing the dry-erase markers with Sharpies."

"Super-lame," Charlotte said, stifling a yawn.

"They will hereby be known as the Devious Four," Lili intoned in a mock-dramatic voice, tapping away on her touch screen. "And don't worry, Mads. My tweet will put them in their place."

"Yeah, we'll see who will be bowing down to who soon enough," Charlotte said grimly, setting her square jaw.

Devious Four Deflower School Property, Emma headlined silently, running her eyes back over the skanky lingerie. The display was tackier than the shark tattoo her last foster brother, Travis, had come home with after a thirty-six-hour drinking binge.

"Whoa," said a familiar voice. Emma turned to see Laurel coming up behind them, her blue cotton dress billowing in the breeze. Her blond hair gleamed in the sunlight, and her mouth was open so wide Emma could see her molars. "That's insane."

At that moment the doors to the school flung open, and Ms. Ambrose, the principal, burst onto the lawn.

The students parted for her—she was making a path straight for Emma and the others. Emma watched helplessly as the woman strode closer and closer. The corners of the principal's lips turned down in a frown. The look in her eyes said, *You've crossed the line one too many times, girls.*

Emma put on her best Sutton Mercer smile. "Hello, Ms. Ambrose," she said sweetly. "Can you believe someone did this?"

The principal ignored her, grabbing Emma's arm in one hand and Laurel's in the other. "Wait!" Laurel cried. "We didn't do this!"

Her cries were drowned out by the stomping feet of two security guards barreling through the crowd. With swift, deft movements, one of the brawny men grabbed Charlotte and Madeline, and the other took the Twitter Twins.

"You don't understand!" Madeline cried weakly.

"We were set up!" Charlotte protested.

Ms. Ambrose rolled her eyes. "You say that *every time,* girls. You're coming with us."

Emma felt her legs move under her as the principal pulled her toward the door. Just before the crowd closed behind her, she glanced over her shoulder and saw the four freshmen staring at them, huge, ecstatic, we-got-away-with-it smiles on their faces. The girls had probably just wanted to make their mark on the school—literally—but the real damage they'd done was to the members of the Lying Game.

Devious Four indeed, I thought angrily. Those bitches were going down.

5

THE DEVIOUS FOUR

Ms. Ambrose's office smelled like sugary donuts mixed with old, mildewed books. The walls were covered with cheaply framed photographs, cheesy motivational posters with eagles soaring over glaciers, and a master's diploma from Arizona State. A pamphlet for an educational conference in Sedona the following Friday sat on the walnut desk, along with several disciplinary files and a red stapler. Principal Ambrose's ergonomic chair was pushed back, unoccupied. She had stepped out of the room for a moment, leaving Emma and the others in the office alone.

The eagle posters sparked a tiny shard of a memory: no

doubt I'd spent lots of time in here. But my other friends—especially Laurel and the Twitter Twins—looked totally spooked. Charlotte was sitting next to Emma, jiggling her thigh in time with the ticking clock on the principal's wall. Madeline and Laurel sat in the two high-backed chairs that faced the desk, staring at their fingernails. The Twitter Twins were squished into an armchair meant for one person, looking like a human yin-yang symbol.

Lili let out a long sigh and hunched forward dramatically, resting her face in her hands. "Does anyone have a paper bag I can breathe into?"

"Calm down," Madeline said with an eye roll. Her porcelain features were set in a stony mask.

"How can you be calm?" Gabby smoothed a wrinkle in her polo shirt. "I swear to God, if this gets in the way of my Ivy-league dreams I don't know what I'll do."

"Gabs, your *grades* will get in the way of your Ivy-league dreams," Charlotte snapped. "And it's not like they can punish us. We didn't even *do* anything."

"But they think we did," Lili moaned.

Charlotte gave her a cold, calculating look. "You wanted into the Lying Game. Sometimes this comes with the territory."

"Perhaps you'd like us to revoke your membership?" Madeline asked.

Gabby opened her mouth quickly. But before she could

say a word, Ms. Ambrose swept back in, a pinched look on her doughy face. She looked eerily like a baseball mitt. Her brown eyes were the color of old, rotten wood. The skin on her face was folded and worn. She wore her frosted blond hair in a feathered, eighties style—probably the last time she'd gone to a hairdresser.

Ms. Ambrose sat heavily back into her chair and stared at all of them. "You girls have spent the last four years turning this school upside down, and I'm putting a stop to it right now." She focused her attention on Emma, licking her thin lips hungrily.

She was probably dying to get her hands on Sutton Mercer. Little did she know that ship had sailed, I thought grimly.

"Ms. Ambrose, we didn't do this," Emma said quickly.

"It was those freshman bitches!" Lili cried.

Ms. Ambrose whirled around to face Lili. "Watch your language, Miss Fiorello."

"Ms. Ambrose," Madeline started. "What Lilianna is trying to say is that—"

The principal held up a pudgy hand. "What *I'm* trying to say is that I know it's you, and the security cameras will show it."

Emma sat back. "What cameras?" she challenged. Hollier was a public school. They barely had a budget for security guards, let alone security systems.

Ms. Ambrose's steely expression wavered slightly, as though she didn't expect Emma to call her bluff.

Emma pushed on. "If you had cameras, you'd know it wasn't us." And if they *did* have cameras, no doubt the Lying Game members would have been suspended long before this, she added to herself, thinking of all the videos of pranks she'd seen on Laurel's computer. Several occurred on campus, and one included hanging the school's American flag upside down on its pole.

Ms. Ambrose pressed her lips together until they almost disappeared. "Either way, once I have proof, I'll have no trouble expelling all of you."

"Well, we look forward to seeing that proof, which you'll have trouble finding, since we didn't do it," Emma shot back, straightening up. "And if that's all, we're late for homeroom."

The others jumped up quickly and followed Emma out the door. "Miss Mercer!" Ms. Ambrose called after her, but Emma kept going, even though her heart was hammering hummingbird-fast in her chest. She figured it was something Sutton would do. And if there was ever a time to show her friends that she was their fearless leader, it was now.

I had to admit I was impressed with Emma's nerve. She was becoming more and more like me by the second.

★ ★ ★

At lunch, Emma sat in the petite redbrick patio courtyard just outside the cafeteria, waiting for Sutton's friends
to arrive. Only seniors and a few select juniors were
allowed to eat there, and even though the temperature
had dropped, the usual suspects were still holding court.
The soccer team sat at the corner table, chowing on
subs. Garrett craned his neck over the goalie's head, making it plain that he was glaring at Emma. Emma flinched
and looked away.

Garrett had had it in for her since the night of
Sutton's eighteenth birthday party, when he'd offered
her his body and she'd blatantly refused. The night
of the Homecoming Dance, he'd cornered her in the
supply room to confront her about dating Ethan—and
her history with Thayer. She didn't have any evidence
that he'd hurt Sutton, but she hadn't ruled him out as a
suspect quite yet. It was possible he'd known all along
that Sutton had been sneaking around with Thayer and
wanted revenge.

It was something I'd thought about, too. Garrett was
a goody-goody, and I couldn't imagine him having the
nerve to kill me, but at this point, I was willing to consider *anyone* a suspect.

"Dining alone?" a voice said, and Emma looked up to

see Charlotte, a cardboard carton containing four hot beverages in hand. Emma breathed in. They smelled like hot chocolate, a nice change from the gallons of coffee Sutton and her friends usually drank.

"Not anymore," Emma said, pushing away her German text.

Charlotte took a seat and pushed her red curls behind her shoulders. "Did you hear that the Twitter Twins got detention?"

"For the prank?"

Charlotte rolled her eyes. "Nah. They got caught tweeting in class. Probably to their dad's lawyer or something."

Emma snorted. "They need to chill."

A squeal sounded across the courtyard. A chubby girl in leggings and Tory Burch flats was pointing at something just out of view. "It's Thayer Vega!"

A hush fell over the courtyard immediately. Charlotte froze, her hot chocolate inches from her lips, and Emma edged out of her seat. There, in the doorway, was Thayer, with Laurel and Madeline at his heels. His dark hair hung shaggily around his eyes and he had on a North Face down vest and broken-in gray corduroys. He moved across the courtyard confidently—or as confidently as someone could move with a limp.

To me, the limp made him even sexier, like he was vulnerable, mortal. Then my gaze slid to Laurel. She smiled up at him flirtatiously, shaking her honey-blond hair free from its ponytail. He looked down at her with affection. *No*, I thought. This was *my* kind of entrance. And Thayer was only supposed to look at *me* like that.

The captain of the girls' soccer team broke the silence. "Thayer Vega for Harvest Dance King!" she whooped. A cheer erupted among the students.

Thayer coughed in embarrassment, then dropped his tray next to Emma's. Emma started in surprise. Why wasn't Thayer sitting with the soccer guys? She glanced at Garrett's table over her shoulder, but none of the boys were even looking Thayer's way. Were they all showing solidarity for Garrett?

As though reading her mind, Thayer nodded at the soccer table. "Apparently I'm not as useful to them now that I can't kick."

She caught the scent of his minty shampoo as he shifted in his seat to face her. The sun reflected in his eyes, turning them a golden brown. Emma drew her bottom lip into her mouth. "How's your first day back?"

"Well, my old soccer buddies aside, I don't think I've ever been so popular," he said with a hint of a smirk. "Maybe I should go missing more often."

Madeline lowered herself into the seat next to Thayer and swatted him. "Don't even joke about that!" Then she narrowed her eyes at Emma, as if to say, *Remember what I told you?*

Emma felt another pair of eyes on her, too: Laurel's. Sutton's sister was glaring fiercely at her, her gaze bouncing from Emma's face to Emma's and Thayer's fingers. Emma hadn't realized they were almost touching. Emma quickly grasped her cup of hot chocolate, angling slightly away from Thayer.

"Where's your *boyfriend*, Sutton?" Laurel said pointedly.

"Taking his mom to the doctor," Emma said coldly. "Where's *your* boyfriend? Have you officially dumped him yet?"

Laurel crunched angrily into a carrot stick, not answering. The other people at the table shifted uncomfortably. Finally, Charlotte cleared her throat. "So, are you two excited for your dad's party on Saturday?"

Madeline launched into a story about her father's disastrous birthday party a few years ago. But before she could get to the punch line, a crackling sound blared from the loudspeaker mounted over the doors.

"Hello, Hollier students," came the gravelly voice. "This is Principal Ambrose. I have an announcement regarding the Harvest Dance next Friday."

Students perked up across the patio, and conversations ceased.

"Due to the recent vandalism to school property," Ms. Ambrose continued, "I regret to inform the student body that the dance has been canceled. Unless the persons responsible step forward, this decision is final."

Everyone collectively gasped. Girls groaned. The soccer table looked pissed. One girl actually started crying. Emma's stomach sank. She thought about the moment when Ethan asked her to the dance, and how excited she'd been to see him in a suit.

"Told you they didn't have cameras," Emma said in a defeated voice.

"*Shit*," Madeline said beneath her breath.

"This is very not good," Laurel said gravely as all heads turned toward Emma, Charlotte, Madeline, and Laurel. The stares weren't friendly. The looks on everyone's faces said *How dare you*. The table of girls next to the Lying Game group stood up in unison and walked away, as though Emma and the others were afflicted with the plague.

The swish of pom-poms filled the air, and three cheerleaders stalked by and leveled their glares on Emma and her friends. "Thanks for ruining *everything*," the tallest one snapped. Then she tossed her hair over her shoulder and walked on.

Charlotte slumped down in her seat. "I haven't been this ostracized since I was the skinniest girl at fat camp."

Laurel nudged Madeline. "Aren't some of those girls in your dance class? Tell them the truth!"

But Madeline's gaze was on something else. Emma swung around. There, sitting just inside the cafeteria, clinking their Diet Cokes and smirking like they'd gotten away with murder, were the Devious Four. Emma tried to give them the nastiest look she could, but the girls just stared back, undaunted.

I couldn't believe the balls these bitches had. Where was the respect?

"We've got to get them," Emma murmured.

"How?" Madeline curled forward over her Hogan bag, looking expectantly at Emma.

"Um," Emma stalled. She racked her brain for a Sutton-worthy idea. "With another prank."

"And, that's my cue to leave," Thayer said under his breath. He slipped his black bag over his shoulder and started across the patio.

A streak of nerves passed through Emma. Lately the Lying Game pranks had been getting out of hand. Some of them, like Gabby disappearing in the desert, had been downright dangerous. "What if it's . . . a *nice* prank?"

Laurel wrinkled her nose. "Why would we be nice to them?"

But an idea was forming in Emma's mind. "Go with me here. Let's throw our *own* dance next Friday—and keep a very tight guest list." She glanced at the girls just inside the cafeteria doors. "We won't invite a certain freshman four, if you know what I mean."

Charlotte let out an excited whoop. "I love it!"

"*Brilliant!*" Madeline cried. "It will make everyone love us again, *and* it excludes the girls that burned us."

I had to admit that I liked it, too. I was impressed my sister thought of it. And I kind of liked that we were going to pull a prank that didn't target anyone for once. From my new lofty vantage point, it didn't exactly feel good to watch how my friends and I used to treat people— and each other. Would things have been different—would *I* have been different—if Emma was in my life before I died? Would she have brought out a better, kinder side of me? Or would being around me have made her as mean as I was?

Charlotte flipped her hair over her shoulder. "I think this calls for a prank-planning session. Hot springs, anyone?"

"Perfect," Madeline said, just as the bell signaling the end of lunch sounded. "Tomorrow night?"

"Done." Emma gathered her books and stuffed them

into Sutton's leather satchel. Right as she was about to slide from the table, she noticed the Devious Four once more. They were staring straight at her, watching her every move like a hawk homing in on its prey.

Look out, Sis. When you're playing with fire, anyone can burn you. Even a freshman.

6

EVIDENCE LOCKER

That afternoon, the sun beat down on the Hollier tennis team as they went through warm-up stretches. Everyone was doing their own versions of yoga poses. Clara bent over in a Downward-Facing Dog position. Charlotte kicked her leg behind her, stretching her quad. Laurel sat a few feet away from everyone else, wrapping sticky white athletic tape around her ankle. She looked lost in thought—probably about Thayer.

Even though phones weren't technically allowed at practice, Emma had Sutton's iPhone in her palms, reading the most recent text from Ethan. SO BUMMED ABOUT THE DANCE, he said.

DON'T BE, Emma wrote back. MY FRIENDS AND I HAVE AN IDEA THAT MAKES UP FOR IT.

BE CAREFUL! Ethan warned. DO YOU REALLY WANT TO GET INTO MORE TROUBLE?

IT'S GOING TO BE GREAT, Emma typed quickly. I PROMISE. HEY, ARE YOU STILL UP FOR THE GAME TONIGHT? There was a boys' soccer game at Wheeler, their rival school, that would clinch their spot in the District Finals. As Sutton, she was expected to go. As Sutton's boyfriend, Ethan was expected to go, too.

I GUESS SO, Ethan wrote back. Emma could feel his hesitation through the phone line. MY FIRST SOCCER GAME . . . AND I'M A SENIOR. LOL.

IF IT MAKES YOU FEEL ANY BETTER, IT'S MY FIRST GAME, TOO, Emma wrote back. I'LL PICK YOU UP AT 7.

"Writing to Ethan?" Charlotte teased, sidling up to Emma and plopping down on the bench.

Emma covered the screen self-consciously. "How'd you know?"

"Because you have a big, dumb, love-struck look on your face." Charlotte nudged her. "Before the dance was canceled, there were rumors that Ethan was going to be voted Harvest King."

Emma's mouth dropped open. "Really?"

"Don't look so surprised. He's dating *you*. Of course

he'd be nominated." Charlotte separated her ponytail down the middle and yanked it tighter.

"Are you ready, Hollier women?" a loud voice boomed.

Everyone looked over to see Coach Maggie in shiny navy blue Umbros and a white collared Hollier tennis shirt, standing with her hands on her hips at the edge of the courts. A couple of girls smirked. Maggie was always calling them "Hollier women," or "women of Hollier," or, once: "women of the racket."

"Today's practice will be a test of sheer will," Maggie went on, pacing along the baseline. "I've pitted each of you against the player with whom your skills are most evenly matched. We'll start with our cocaptains, Nisha and Sutton." She paused dramatically as though expecting a round of applause. When she didn't get one, she tossed two fuzzy tennis balls in Nisha's direction. "Court six, ladies," she said, gesturing to the court farthest from where the team sat.

Charlotte gave Emma a sympathetic glance—normally being paired with Nisha wasn't something Sutton exactly celebrated.

Emma shrugged. "She's okay," she murmured.

Charlotte looked surprised, but didn't say anything.

Nisha glanced sideways at Emma as they made their way across the court, like she was trying to gauge whether she and Emma would slip back into rival mode, or if their truce from the previous night would hold.

HIDE AND SEEK

Emma gave Nisha a reassuring smile, hoping to put the girl at ease. "Can we stretch some more first?" she asked. "I'm sore after last night."

Nisha sighed with relief. "Me, too."

A series of footfalls sounded behind them, and the boys' soccer team thundered past for their warm-up laps around the field. "Hey, Nisha," Garrett called.

"Hey," Nisha said faintly, waving back.

Then Garrett noticed Emma next to her. His expression soured.

There was an uncomfortable pause, and the girls walked quietly for a few seconds. "So you *are* still seeing Garrett?" Emma asked in as friendly a voice as she could muster, thinking about how Nisha had avoided the question last night.

Nisha adjusted the strap of her dark purple tank. "We were never really seeing each other," she said. "He only went with me to get back at you."

Then Emma remembered the real answer she had wanted from Nisha last night. "Can I ask you a weird question?"

Nisha put a hand on the hip of her neatly pleated white shorts and waited.

Emma swallowed hard. "Are you sure my sister was at the back-to-school sleepover the whole night?"

Nisha's eyes flickered back and forth. "Why?"

"I just think she was somewhere else and lying to me about it. Sister stuff," Emma said vaguely. "I'm not going to get you in trouble or anything. But if you remember something, please tell me."

A few beads of sweat appeared on Nisha's brow. Finally she let out a sigh. "I suppose I'm not a hundred percent sure she was there the *whole* night."

Emma's heart thumped. "Was she there when you woke up in the morning?"

Nisha pushed a strand of hair off her face. "Well, no."

"Was she there for breakfast or anything?" Emma asked, clutching her racket.

Nisha raised one shoulder, then let it drop.

"So she *wasn't* there the whole night," Emma said. "But you said she was."

Nisha's eyes flashed. "God, Sutton. I was trying to piss you off, okay? I was mad that you told Laurel not to hang out with me. I wanted you to know that she went behind your back and did it anyway."

Emma barely heard her. She stepped back and turned to face Laurel, who was dueling Charlotte on court one. Laurel smashed a lob overhead, sending the ball sailing past Charlotte's outstretched racket. She did a happy victory dance like she was a normal, ordinary teenager. But Nisha had just given her confirmation. Laurel never went back to the sleepover that night. Suddenly, it felt like the air had been sucked from Emma's lungs. She bent at the waist, staring down at the baked clay ground.

"Hey, are you okay?" Nisha's shadow loomed over Emma. "You look like you're going to pass out."

"Um, I just . . . need water," Emma stammered. "I'll be right back."

She took off in the direction of the school, doing her best to look casual. She pushed through the double doors of the girls' locker room, the smell of plastic and stale bread making her feel sick. Half a chocolate-chip cookie was squished along the wooden bench lining the lockers. She checked the stalls, relieved that they were empty, then found Laurel's locker, which was decorated with shooting stars, gold-foil tennis rackets, and Laurel's name in purple bubble letters. She touched the lock and twisted the combination to zero. *I just need to find something*, she thought manically. *Anything.*

I held my breath. This seemed dangerous. I only hoped she knew what she was doing.

Emma used the toe of her sneaker to pound the base of the locker—Alex had taught her at their old high school in Henderson that if you turned a lock to zero and kicked it, the lock would open. The locker creaked, then burst open. *Score.*

Several notebooks were stashed at the bottom, along with a thick chemistry textbook. On the top shelf was a tube of melon-scented deodorant. Emma yanked Laurel's brown leather bag from the metal hook and opened it like a kid tearing open a Christmas present. Laurel's iPhone, safe in its pink neoprene case, was in the side pocket, amid gum wrappers and ballpoint pens. Emma set the purse back inside the locker and pushed the door closed in case anyone came in. The last thing she needed was someone telling Laurel they'd seen her sister snooping through her stuff.

Then with trembling fingers, she scrolled through the texts, from the most recent to ones from more than a month ago. Just this Monday, she'd written to Thayer: I'M GLAD WE TALKED. Another to Thayer earlier on Monday: IT'S IMPORTANT YOU DON'T TELL ANYONE.

Other than a few WHERE ARE YOUs, there was no correspondence when Thayer was in rehab. But even Laurel's texts to Charlotte and Madeline were oddly cryptic—things like SORRY I HAD TO BAIL BUT SOMETHING CAME UP and I NEED TO TALK TO YOU, but never any details. It was almost like she expected someone to snoop.

Emma took out Sutton's iPhone and snapped a photo of the texts—she could decipher them later. Finally, she scrolled to August thirty-first, the day of Sutton's death. Laurel had sent a bunch of texts that day, but only one to Sutton, time stamped 10:43 P.M. When Emma read it, her throat caught, and her vision went fuzzy.

THE NEXT TIME I SEE YOU, YOU'RE DEAD.

Emma slumped against the locker stall, her hand over her mouth.

Over her shoulder, I read the text again and again, the black type silhouetted against the green text bubble. Suddenly the screen felt too bright, the neon glow taking over my entire vision. And just like that, something shifted in my mind and I was sucked into a full-blown memory.

7

CAN YOU HEAR ME NOW?

The headlights of Laurel's Jetta flash as she makes a U-turn across the dirt road. Jealousy surges through me as her car speeds off, taking Thayer farther and farther away from me. My boyfriend is seriously hurt and my sister, who would freak out if she knew the truth about me and Thayer, is the one there to hold his hand. I should be the one taking him to a hospital. Not her.

Brushing off my clothes, I stand up from my position in the shrubs. To protect my secret relationship with Thayer, I had crouched in the bushes when she arrived. But from the glare she sent in my direction, I could tell she knew I was there. I can only hope she hasn't figured out why.

I glance around, getting my bearings. A dark mountain looms behind me. Next to me is a sign that reads PLEASE DON'T FEED THE SNAKES, and off to my left is a tourist train car bearing a sign that says SABINO CANYON RIDES FROM 10 A.M. TO 5 P.M! CHUGGA CHUGGA CHOO CHOO! I'm one hundred yards away from Sabino Canyon's dusty, empty parking lot, and just feet from where someone hit Thayer with my car.

I still can't believe how this night turned out. My mind replays the events of the evening over and over, like a horror movie stuck on repeat. I recall my giddiness as I picked up Thayer at the bus station and drove him to the overlook in Sabino Canyon, where my dad used to take me bird watching when I was little. I feel my terror as Thayer and I ran through the canyon, some unknown pursuer fast on our heels. I hear the roar of my Volvo tearing across the pavement and crashing into Thayer. The only thing I can't see is the face behind the wheel, the face of the person who stole my car and tried to run us down. There's no way it was an accident. But was the person gunning for Thayer—or for me?

I look up to the night sky hoping to see some kind of sign, some kind of message that assures me everything will be okay. But a shiver crawls along my spine and I know everything is not okay. Thayer is seriously hurt, and I still don't know how a night that had started with such romantic promise had devolved into this.

A motorbike's engine chokes in the distance, breaking me from my thoughts and reminding me that I need to get the hell out of this canyon.

Dried leaves crackle as I emerge from the thicket and send little brown birds fluttering into the sky, calling to each other with soft, squeaking noises, as if discussing where to settle next. I pull out my phone. Maybe I can't tell the cops what happened to Thayer—no one can know he came back to Tucson to see me—but I can report my car stolen. I just hope they don't send Detective Quinlan. He was so mad after our last prank that I think he'd arrest me just for the hell of it.

I'm about to dial 911 when I realize I don't have service. Shit. I curse my provider—Thayer's phone worked when he called Laurel to pick him up, but of course the canyon has interrupted my signal.

A cloud passes over the moon. A coyote wails in the distance. The reality of the situation crashes around me hard. Someone stole my car, and now I'm out in the middle of nowhere with no way to call for help.

Nisha's house isn't far from here, and I know the rest of the tennis team is there. But I can't go back to the parking lot in case that lunatic who hit Thayer is still out there, waiting for me. I'll need to take a different route, one that winds around the base of the canyon. The wind howls as I set out. The path narrows and the trees thicken above my head. The brush along the sides of the trail claws at my ankles like fingernails, ripping the skin there and drawing blood. I keep going, knowing I won't be safe until I reach a populated area.

A screech of tires sounds in the distance, followed by a crash. I whirl around and stumble over a root sticking up in the path, *breaking my fall with my palms. Bits of gravel groove into my skin, stinging like I'd just dried my hands with sandpaper. My cell phone falls out of my pocket and lands in the dirt, the screen lighting up with an incoming call.*

Instead of sobbing with pain, I cry out with relief. I have cell service again. This nightmare is one phone call away from being over. But then I notice the number on the screen.

I let out a long breath and reject Laurel's call. I can't deal with her anger right now—or her questions. A second later my phone buzzes with a text.

THE NEXT TIME I SEE YOU, YOU'RE DEAD.

Way to overreact, Sis, *I think, and press* DELETE.

8

A BRUSH WITH DANGER

"What are you doing?"

Emma's head snapped up. When she saw the figure standing at the end of the aisle, backlit by the sun streaming through the frosted windows, her blood went cold. It was Laurel.

I waved my useless arms, wishing I could yank Emma away to safety. All I could see was the memory that had just been given back to me. That dark, spooky canyon. That text appearing on my phone. I'd dismissed it so carelessly at the time—as sisters, Laurel and I had probably threatened to kill each other hundreds of times. But given my current state, I had to consider that when Laurel wrote that text, it wasn't just a passing expression of anger and frustration. Maybe she meant what she said. What if she *had* dropped Thayer off at the hospital and come back to kill me? It had been so dark on that mountain. So secluded. Anything could have happened, and no one would have heard.

Pushing to her feet, Emma shoved Laurel's cell phone into the pocket of her shorts, praying that this wasn't the moment that someone decided to send Sutton's sister a text—Laurel had a very unique and very recognizable monkey squawk as her text ringtone. She kept Sutton's phone in her other hand. "What are *you* doing?" Emma shot back, trying to harness Sutton's brash, back-off attitude.

Laurel's eyes flicked over Emma as if she knew she'd caught Emma doing something illicit and was trying to figure out what it was. "I heard you walked off the court because you weren't feeling well," she said in an even voice. "Like a *good* sister I came to check on you."

Sutton's phone was beginning to feel slippery in Emma's palm. "I was a little dizzy," she said, wary of Laurel's intense gaze on her. "I came in here to get my extra water bottle and decided to sit for a minute."

"Really?" Laurel asked, rocking back and forth on her heels. She said it overemphatically, and the weird smile on her face broadened. "Funny that you're in front of *my* locker, then. Looking for something?"

Emma's mind raced, flashing through the times Sutton's killer had attacked her. The hands strangling her from behind. The light crashing down inches from her head, the writing on that chalkboard telling her to stop digging. If Laurel followed through with what she said in her text, then she was dangerous—*really* dangerous. And here Emma was, digging again—and finding a piece of evidence that could hurt Laurel. Emma looked around the cavernous locker room. If she screamed, would anyone hear her?

When Laurel stepped forward, Emma flinched, certain Sutton's sister was making her move. But Laurel slid past her, spun the code to her locker, and opened the door. Emma's heart pounded in her ears as Laurel rifled through her purse. Her eyes were on Emma the whole time. *She's looking for her phone,* Emma thought. *She knows it won't be there, because she knows I have it. She's just doing this to make me sweat.*

"Well?" Laurel finally said, pulling out a hairbrush and raking it through her long blond ponytail. "I mean, I know I'm fascinating and everything—Thayer definitely thinks so." A small smile flitted along her lips when she said Thayer's name. "But shouldn't you get your water and head back to practice?"

"Oh. Of course," Emma said, but she didn't move. It felt like Laurel's phone, nestled in Emma's back pocket, was on fire. Then Laurel turned her back to get a drink from the water fountain, and Emma quickly tossed the iPhone in Laurel's bag. Amazingly, Laurel didn't seem to notice.

Emma turned on her heel and scuttled around the corner to Sutton's locker. Her fingers shook as she worked the combination and opened the door. She rummaged around for a moment, pretending to search, and retrieved the bottle of Evian that was thankfully sitting on the upper shelf. She tipped it back and guzzled it down, but the liquid did nothing to quench her thirst.

When she looked up, Laurel was standing at the end of the aisle, staring at her phone with wide eyes. Emma nearly screamed. For an agonizingly long moment Emma couldn't remember if she'd clicked off Laurel's text to Sutton and returned to the phone's main screen.

"Huh," Laurel said, frowning.

"What?" Emma asked shakily.

"I could have sworn I put this in the side pocket of my purse," Laurel said slowly.

Alarms blared in Emma's head. *She knows you were digging! Run away, now!* But her sneakers felt nailed to the floor. "I have no idea where you put your phone," she mumbled, the words jammed in her throat.

"Of course you don't," Laurel simpered, rolling her eyes. She slipped the phone in her pocket, then sauntered toward Emma, her eyes blazing. Heat seemed to radiate from her body, her limbs coiled to strike.

"*Boo*," Laurel whispered, touching Emma's chest. Emma screamed and recoiled, shielding her body with her hands and shutting her eyes tight.

When she opened them again, Laurel was snickering. "*Someone's* jumpy," she said as she sauntered past. The door hinges squeaked as she slammed out of the locker room.

Emma left the locker room, too, standing just outside the doorway. Soft *thwaps* from the tennis balls on the court filled the air as she watched Laurel trot across the practice fields and rejoin the team at the tennis courts. She was smiling from ear to ear, as though she hadn't just acted completely diabolical and crazy a moment before. But Emma knew better.

And I did, too. Laurel was onto her. And my sister had better watch her back.

9

THAT'S ONE WAY TO WIN

A few hours later, Emma steered into the driveway of Ethan's bungalow, which was located in a development across the street from Sabino Canyon. It was the smallest house on the block—Nisha's, which was next door, was more than twice the size—and had definitely seen better days. Black paint flaked from the shutters, and there was a tiny tear in the screen door, which hung crooked on its hinges.

She opened the car door and made her way onto Ethan's front porch. Crickets sounded from the wooded area behind Ethan's house, their steady humming ringing in Emma's ears. She raised her hand to press the doorbell, but drew back when she heard a crash.

"Damn it, Ethan!" a woman's voice rang out just inside the door. A figure passed by the screen, not noticing Emma on the porch. "Didn't I ask you to vacuum yesterday?"

Emma drew away from the doorbell. But before she could scamper off the porch, footsteps pounded, and a tall woman appeared in the foyer.

"What do *you* want?" The woman's blue-flowered dress hung loose over her skeletal frame and freckles spotted her pale skin. Thin, mouse-colored brown hair was pulled back in a messy ponytail, and tiny fly-aways hung in her eyes.

I had a feeling I knew her. But I had no idea why. Ethan and I hadn't exactly hung out at each other's houses.

"Uh, hi," Emma squeaked, peering at Ethan's mom through the screen. Mrs. Landry hadn't opened it for her. "I'm Sutton," she went on, shifting her weight. "I'm here to pick up Ethan for the soccer game."

"I know who you are," the woman said bitingly.

There were more footsteps, and Ethan appeared behind his mother, looking mortified. "Uh, see you, Mom. I'll be back at nine."

He pushed around his mother and slipped onto the porch. Mrs. Landry's top lip formed a thin, unmoving line. "It was nice to see you," Emma said meekly. Mrs. Landry just sniffed, and walked away. The door slammed loudly behind her.

"Is everything okay?" Emma asked quietly.

Ethan shrugged. "She's just in one of her moods."

Emma touched his arm sympathetically. His mom had had cancer, and Mr. Landry went AWOL during the chemo treatments. Even though Mrs. Landry was in remission, she'd never fully recovered emotionally, and she expected Ethan to take care of almost every household chore.

Ethan slid into the passenger seat and buckled his belt, and Emma turned on the engine. "So can I see the text?" Ethan asked quietly.

Emma nodded. Idling in the driveway, she pulled Sutton's cell phone from her bag, and showed him the picture she'd taken of Laurel's screen. After she'd found the text, she'd called Ethan immediately to tell him about it. His brow furrowed as he studied the photo. "Wow," he whispered.

"I know," Emma said, looking at it, too. *The next time I see you, you're dead.*

Ethan sat back in the bucket seat, the vintage leather crunching beneath him. "So you think Laurel killed Sutton in some kind of a jealous rage, because she was with Thayer?"

If I could have shivered, I would have. I thought about the call Thayer made to Laurel just after he'd been hit. She'd arrived so quickly, almost like she'd been waiting around the corner. Thayer had said someone was chasing us in the canyon—was it Laurel? Had she followed me and Thayer that night and realized we were dating behind her back? Had she stolen my car and tried to hit me—only to accidentally hit the boy she loved instead? Had she then come back to the canyon to finish me off?

Emma shifted into reverse and turned out of the driveway. "Maybe. Love can make people do crazy things. Thayer's hot. And obviously a charmer."

As soon as the words were out of her mouth, Emma regretted them. But Ethan just nodded thoughtfully. "She always used to follow him around—to the point that even I noticed it," he said with a wry chuckle. "It seemed like puppy love at the time, but if you're right about what happened, then it was much more sinister than that."

Emma paused at the stop sign and watched as cars whizzed past on the main road. "How do you think she did it? Killed Sutton, I mean." The words tasted sour on her tongue. It was one thing to talk about Sutton being gone, but it felt so macabre to talk about the specifics of her death.

I flinched as I considered my final moments. My most recent memories were of my final night on earth, but each time they cut off so abruptly. My death was *so close*, and I kept waiting to see how it all ended. I wanted to see it . . .

and I also didn't. Regaining my last moments meant that I'd have to experience them all over again. I'd be forced to watch the life drain out of me. And I'd *feel* it. I had to wonder if there was some reason I *hadn't* seen it yet. Maybe when whatever cosmic force was keeping me suspended here in the in-between finally let me remember my death, I would die all over again. I'd see my killer, take my last breath, and explode into the ether, gone as swiftly and soundlessly as a bird taking flight.

Then another thought struck me hard, chilling me to my core. All my memories were sparked by things Emma uncovered—Laurel's text, Lili's threat about the train prank, Thayer's return. What if my last memory came to me because my killer was doing to Emma exactly what had been done to me? What if we only discovered the truth when it was too late?

Ethan placed his hand on Emma's knee. "I don't know. She did try to strangle Sutton in the snuff video. And if she drove back to find Sutton, she could have used her car or some kind of weapon. It will be hard to know unless we . . ." Ethan's voice trailed off. He cleared his throat gruffly. "Unless we . . . *find* her."

"True," Emma murmured, a knot forming in the pit of her stomach at Ethan's words. She took a deep breath, stopping behind a chugging motorcycle at a traffic light. "I just need to get Thayer alone for a minute so I can ask him if Laurel stayed at the hospital with him all night. If she was there, she's in the clear, but if not . . ."

She let her sentence hang in the air, and they drove the rest of the way in silence. A few minutes later, they pulled into the Wheeler parking lot. Emma had just been here a few weeks ago for a tennis match. The school was Hollier's main rival, but it was a little more run-down, with chipped columns holding up sagging portico. To the left of the school, floodlights illuminated the soccer field. The players were warming up in tracksuits—maroon and yellow for Wheeler and forest green for Hollier.

They got out of the car and strolled through the busy parking lot toward the field. The air smelled of concession stand hot dogs and soft pretzels, and a bunch of kids were milling around the gates. When they noticed Emma and Ethan, they turned and stared. A couple girls nudged one another and smiled at Ethan.

Emma slipped her hand into Ethan's. His palms were sweaty. This was his first public appearance as Sutton Mercer's boyfriend.

"It'll be okay," she whispered.

"I know," Ethan said stiffly, quickly glancing at his reflection in the chrome siding of one of the food carts just past the entrance. That was when Emma noticed how meticulously he'd dressed tonight—his jeans looked new, his blue polo perfectly matched his eyes, and he'd shaved, using the Kiehl's aftershave she'd bought for him this past weekend. It was cute that he was so eager to make a good impression.

Even though they were at Wheeler, it felt like all of Hollier had turned out for the match. The stands were full of kids in green, who were stamping their feet and singing the school song. Emma looked for Madeline's black hair and Charlotte's shock of red, but she didn't see them. "That's weird," she murmured. "They told me they'd be on the top row."

"Maybe they're busy planning another prank on us," Ethan mumbled under his breath.

"Ha, ha, very funny," Emma said. The Lying Game had trapped Emma and Ethan in an abandoned house together last week. "Maybe they'll lock us in a bathroom this time."

Ethan wrinkled his nose. "Hopefully not the guys' locker room. That place smells like ass."

"Maybe the massage room for the sports teams," Emma teased. "With our own personal masseuse."

Ethan broke into a smile. "Now *that* I could get behind."

There was an empty spot at the top, and Emma pulled Ethan up the metal steps. A few kids moved over to make room for them to sit. One girl with a short bob lifted her phone, pretending to text, but Emma could tell she'd snapped Ethan's picture. Two freshman girls a few rows down giggled and pointed Ethan's way.

Emma nudged his side. "Don't look now, but I think you have the beginnings of a fan club."

Ethan flushed. "Yeah, right."

His bashfulness didn't fool me, though. As Ethan ran a hand through his inky dark hair, I caught a trace of a smile on his face. Was it possible Loner Boy was enjoying the new attention? I always thought it was telling that the only people who railed against popularity were the unpopular ones. Who *wouldn't* want to be adored?

A ref blew his whistle, and the two teams ran back to their benches to talk to the coaches before the game started. The scent of yellow mustard tickled Emma's nose, and a soft breeze whispered across the back of her neck.

Ethan slipped an arm around her waist and pulled her close. "Are you cold?"

"Maybe a little," Emma said.

"Sutton used to say night games were her favorite," Ethan murmured so no one else could hear. "She said there was something really sexy about playing under the stars."

Emma twisted around to face him. "Really?"

Ethan tucked a dark curl behind his ear. "I overheard her say that once in the halls. I guess it stuck with me."

Emma pulled in her bottom lip, feeling unexpectedly

jealous. It seemed like every guy at school had had a crush on Sutton. Had Ethan, too? She knew it was ridiculous to be jealous of her dead twin sister, but she couldn't help but wonder, sometimes, if Ethan saw something in Sutton that he didn't see in her. "Is there anything else about her that stuck with you?" she asked quietly.

"I've told you everything." Ethan curled his fingers around Emma's. "I wish I knew more."

Emma let out a breath. "So do I."

"Sutton!" Gabby cried. She and Lili were making their way up the bleachers, wearing matching HOLLIER SOCCER GROUPIE T-shirts. Charlotte, Madeline, Thayer, and Laurel followed a few steps behind. Thayer wore his old soccer jersey. Somewhat ironically he was number thirteen.

"Hey!" Emma said, waving them toward her. All she had to do was glance at the kids around them, and a whole slew of girls and guys got up, no questions asked, and moved down several rows. It was insane having that kind of power, especially when in her previous life, she would have been the one scurrying away.

Ethan watched as everyone climbed up the bleachers. "Let the games begin," he murmured under his breath.

Lili reached the top and twirled around, showing off the back of her hot pink T-shirt, which read GET CRASS ON THE GRASS. "Like 'em? We had them custom-made."

"You can't find something this authentic in the school

store," Gabby added. She was wearing an identical shirt, except in neon yellow.

Madeline slid in next to Ethan on the other side from Emma. "Hey, Poet," she said, nudging him in the ribs.

Emma avoided eye contact with Thayer, willing him not to sit in the empty spot next to her, but to her chagrin, he sank down and said hello. Emma's fingers tightened around Ethan's, as if to say, *It's okay.* Luckily Ethan squeezed back and gave her a small smile.

Laurel looked sourly at Thayer and Emma, then took the seat on the other side of Thayer.

"How's Hollier soccer's number-one fan?" Thayer asked, fake-punching Emma in the arm.

"Uh, still kicking," Emma said, realizing how lame she sounded.

Thayer gave her a stern look. "You aren't going to cheer for Hollier now that I'm off the team, are you? Personally, I'm hoping Wheeler wins."

Emma frowned good-naturedly. "Traitor."

Thayer laughed louder than necessary, and he stared at Emma with twinkling, unblinking hazel eyes. Emma felt Ethan's fingers slip from hers.

I felt a little hurt, too. Thayer was looking at my twin the same way he looked at me in the memories I had of our time together. I wanted to put my hands on his shoulders, to make him see *me*, not Emma. If he loved me so much, how come he couldn't see that the girl he'd fallen for wasn't the person sitting next to him?

Charlotte took a huge, floppy red hat out of her purse and pulled it low over her forehead. Madeline looked at her and giggled. "*What* are you doing?"

Charlotte pulled the brim lower over her forehead. "I'm sick of everyone staring at me because of that stupid Devious Four prank. Tad Phelps actually had the nerve to ask which bras were mine. Seven people unfriended me on Facebook, and no one was afraid of me in debate. Before, they all used to cower when I took the podium, never wanting to argue with me for fear I might retaliate by pranking them. Today one girl questioned my use of the phrase 'moral character' given the, quote, 'recent vandalism to school property.'"

Emma looked out over the bleachers, and sure enough, at least fifteen different people were peering at the Lying Game members and whispering angrily.

"Throwing the dance isn't enough. We need to prove that we didn't do this," Charlotte said.

Laurel sighed dramatically. "I can't believe I'm saying this, but I actually wish the school *did* have security cameras. Then we could show everyone it wasn't us."

Ethan looked up, a hesitant expression on his face. "You know, there are traffic cameras on the corner next to school."

Laurel narrowed her eyes. "So?"

"So," Ethan continued, "I got a ticket once for running the light there, and they sent me my ticket along with a photo. I could see the front of the school in the background. Maybe those traffic cams caught the vandalism to the school." Ethan shrugged.

"Seriously?" Madeline's eyes lit up. But then she visibly deflated. "How could we ever get access to that though?"

Ethan licked his lips. "Well . . . the camera feed goes to an online site that you can access remotely and I'm pretty good with computers. I, uh, hacked into the site at the time to see if I could get the ticket erased." His cheeks reddened visibly. "I couldn't, but I did notice they kept an archive of the video footage. The password's probably changed, but with a little time, I think I could figure out how to get back in."

"OMG, that would be amazing!" Charlotte squealed.

"That's badass, Ethan," Madeline said admiringly. "I had no idea you had it in you."

The other Lying Game girls cheered and smiled. Only one person looked less than delighted: Thayer. He kept his gaze on the field, even though play hadn't started yet. "Like it's really that hard to get ahold of surveillance footage," he said under his breath, in a voice only Emma could hear. She pretended not to notice.

Emma turned to Ethan. "Are you sure you want to do that?" The last thing she wanted was for Ethan to get in trouble just to make Sutton's friends like him.

Ethan shrugged. "It's not a big deal. Honest."

Suddenly, a shadow fell over Emma. A girl with dark, curly hair in a side ponytail stood in the aisle. Tiny yellow shorts barely covered her thin thighs, and a white T-shirt showed off the outline of her bra. It took Emma only a few seconds to realize it was one of the members of the Devious Four—Bethany something.

"Hi, Ethan," Bethany said, staring at him and only him. She hitched her shorts even higher.

Ethan blushed, clearly not used to the attention. "Um, hi?"

I rolled my eyes. I was dead and practically memory-less, but even I knew that you never, ever talk to a freshman. You pretended you were too busy to realize they exist, even if you were related to them.

"What are you up to this weekend?" Bethany asked.

Madeline's and Laurel's eyes widened. Lili and Gabby already had their phones out, texting furiously.

"Um . . ." Ethan stalled, glancing at Emma.

It was all Emma could do to not laugh. "He's hanging out with me," she said, looping her arm in Ethan's elbow.

Madeline leaned in. "Why? Does your mom need someone to babysit you?"

Bethany's cheeks flushed scarlet. She slunk away back to her friends, who surrounded her and started whispering.

Charlotte shook her head. "We definitely need that video footage."

"Agreed," Emma said. "Those girls need to go down."

"Consider it done," Ethan answered.

"Our hero," Madeline swooned.

Thayer looked more and more annoyed. He leaned over and stared at Ethan. "Landry, when did you become the man?"

For a second, Ethan looked caught off guard. Then he took a deep breath. "I guess when I started dating the hottest girl in school," he said smoothly.

Thayer focused his brown eyes on Emma, like he was looking at her for the first time that night. "Yeah, can't argue with you there," he said in a wistful tone.

Next to him, Laurel choked on the Diet Coke she was drinking. Thayer spun around instantly and clapped her on the back. "Are you okay?"

Laurel nodded frantically, but she couldn't breathe for a few more seconds. "Could you get me water?" Laurel spluttered, her eyes tearing up.

"Sure." Thayer struggled to get up, then limped down the bleachers.

Laurel kept coughing until he was out of sight, then

calmly took another sip of her soda, angling a sidelong glance at Emma. It was a look that said, *You're not the only one who has him eating out of your hand.*

To me, there was something extra to the look, too. It also said, *Stay away. Or else.*

~ 10 ~

SMOKING GUN

People in the Mercers' neighborhood took Hollier soc-cer seriously. Following the school's victory, horns were honking down the street, and the Wessmans, who lived two doors away, had put a Hollier banner on their garage.

Emma pulled into the driveway and heard a *ping* on her phone. It was Ethan. TONIGHT WAS UNEXPECTEDLY FUN, he wrote. OR IN THE WORDS OF THE DAILY EMMA: SHY BOY SCORES BIG AT SOCCER GAME.

Emma flushed, loving that Ethan had picked up on her headline habit and was writing some of his own. NOT TOO BAD, RIGHT? she typed back, feeling a warm, happy sensation all over. Besides the minor blip with Thayer, Ethan had been awesome: He'd charmed Sutton's friends and even made a couple of hilarious jokes. By the looks Madeline and Charlotte had given her at the end of the game, Emma knew they'd accepted him. It was nice to know Ethan had accepted them, too.

Emma cut the engine and looked around. Surprisingly, she'd beat Laurel back, even though Emma had driven Ethan home after the game. The Mercer parents' cars weren't there either, and though Grandma's car was parked outside the garage, the house was dark.

She stepped through the front door and fumbled for the light. Her footsteps echoed loudly in the silent house. She made her way into the kitchen, where moonlight spilled through the French doors and cast long shadows over the wooden table. She'd come home to plenty of empty houses, but the Mercers' felt oddly cavernous and lonely tonight. She realized with a jolt just how much she'd gotten used to Mrs. Mercer greeting her with a warm hello.

Emma was about to switch on the light when she saw the burning orange glow of a cigarette in the backyard. Her heart picked up speed. A few weeks back, when Ethan had taken her to a gallery opening, they'd been sitting outside on a bench when she'd noticed a dark shape smoking just feet from them, listening to every word they said. The figure had vanished before Emma could see who it was.

Emma let out a low whistle for Drake. Soon enough, she heard the Great Dane ambling into the kitchen. Drake glanced at her with wide eyes. Her fingers were shaky as she ushered him toward the back door—as nervous as she was around the enormous dog, she was more scared of the smoker outside.

"Come on, boy," she soothed as she stepped through the French doors. Her heart lurched when she saw a dark shape reclined in a lawn chair. A curl of smoke wound to the trees, as eerie as a witch's bent finger.

"Sutton?" a familiar raspy voice said.

Emma blinked, her eyes adjusting to the darkness. "*Grandma.*" She let go of Drake's collar and he trotted across the lawn to sniff a cluster of azaleas.

"Who did you think it was? God?" Grandma Mercer waved her cigarette, motioning Emma forward. "Sit down." Grandma Mercer made room for Emma on the end of her dark green lawn chair.

Emma reluctantly sat. To her surprise, Grandma proffered her pack of Merits. "Want one?"

Emma's nose wrinkled. She'd always hated the smell of cigarette smoke. But would Sutton have said yes? "Um, I have a sore throat," she lied. Then she cocked her head. "Why aren't you with Mom and Dad?"

"They were meeting up with the Finches," Sutton's grandmother said, then made a face. "It's such a chore seeing those people. They're always trying to set me up with that awful woman's widowed father. I may be old, but I can find my own dates, thank you very much."

She pinched her cigarette between wrinkled fingers and leveled a long look at Emma. "Sooo," she said slowly, stretching the word out. "Are you really not going to say anything about my—what did you call it last time? 'Filthy little habit that will kill you and age your skin prematurely'?"

Emma laughed out loud. That did sound like something her twin would say—and it was nice to know Sutton wasn't a smoker either. "Nah. I've turned over a new leaf. Live and let live. Or in your case, live until smoking kills you," she said with a wry smile.

Grandma Mercer tapped the ash in a glass she was using as an ashtray. "Sounds good to me. So, Sutton. How's the college search going?" She crossed her legs. "Are you even *going* to college next year?"

"Um," Emma stalled. Something about the question hit her in the gut and she suddenly found it hard to breathe. She'd never seen anything in Sutton's belongings having to do with college visits or applications. Sutton had all the opportunities in the world, and yet she wasn't taking advantage of any of them.

Hey, not all of us were made for college. Maybe I had plans to become a big Hollywood actress.

"I'm just trying to keep my options open," Emma finally said. "But I'm applying to loads of good schools."

"Really?" Grandma Mercer asked, cocking a silver eyebrow. "Are you planning to stay in Arizona?"

"The U of A is good," she said quietly. Ironically, the University of Arizona was one of the colleges she had begun applying to back when she lived in Vegas. They offered a lot of scholarships, and she liked their program in journalism. But the financial aid forms had to be way past due by now. Would she ever get to go back to that old life? Or would she have to apply to schools as Sutton Mercer? *Could* she do something like that? Living in Sutton's room and taking her high school classes was one thing. But attending college on the Mercers' dime, continuing to pretend she was Sutton in the dorms, felt different somehow. And the idea that Sutton's murder would still be unsolved by then was unfathomable.

Grandma wrinkled her nose. "The U of A has a good sorority life, you mean. Life's more than partying, you know."

Emma stared at her sandals. "Trust me. I know."

Grandma Mercer tapped her cigarette on the lawn

chair's handrail, a pensive look on her lined face. "Your father used to love a good party," she said, sighing. "He's a California boy at heart. But he and your mother quieted down quite a bit when they moved to Tucson." She sniffed. "Of course, his job was worth relocating for."

"They lived in California before Tucson?" Emma asked, unable to hide her surprise. The Mercers had never said anything either way, but they were so entrenched in the community here she'd just assumed they'd been here forever.

Grandma gave her a crazy look. "Well of course they did. They moved here just after they adopted you."

"Oh, right. Duh," Emma said faintly. It was strange to think that they'd once had an entirely different life.

Grandma sighed. "I've always missed them being right down the road from me. We used to have so much fun when Sutton was still alive."

Emma's heart clenched. Had she heard the old woman right?

I waited with bated breath. Grandma *had* said Sutton. *Me.*

"My sister loved babies," Grandma Mercer went on, her thin lips breaking into a grin. "And she especially loved you. She fawned over you. Called you her little namesake."

Emma's eyes flicked back and forth as the words slowly

sank in. The Sutton Grandma was talking about wasn't her twin. Sutton was named after Grandma Mercer's sister, her great-aunt.

Grandma reached for her martini glass and took a long sip. "If we lived closer, I could've kept a better eye on you—and kept you out of trouble. Your parents were always far too lenient. A few more weekends with me would have knocked the sass right out of you." She glanced at Emma. But after a moment, her eyes softened and she laid her hand over Emma's. Emma smiled, not expecting this tiny gesture of kindness.

Grandma pursed her lips, like there was something more she wanted to say but couldn't quite find the words. "Anyway," she said, her voice stern again as she removed her hand.

"Anyway," Emma echoed, feeling awkward once more.

Drake raised his head and stared at the door, letting out a low whine. Emma swung around to follow his gaze. Laurel stood just behind the French doors leading into the kitchen, watching Emma and Grandma.

Grandma Mercer waved. "Guess your sister's home."

Caught, Laurel tossed a casual wave back, then retreated from sight. A moment later the light in her bedroom window snapped on.

Grandma Mercer tutted, then stubbed out her

cigarette. "I hope Laurel didn't see the smoke. Unlike you, I can't trust her to keep a secret."

Emma watched Laurel's shadow moving around in the bedroom. "Actually, Laurel's got a few secrets of her own," she murmured. "You'd be surprised what she's capable of."

Like murdering her own sister, I thought grimly.

⁓ 11 ⁓

TOO HOT TO HANDLE

The next evening, Emma stood in the parking lot of Clayton Resort. The low-lying, ultramodern red clay buildings were all lit up, seamlessly melting into the mountain backdrop. All around her was an undulating, impossibly green golf course, the flags rippling in the slight wind. Several sprinklers came on at once, misting the grassy areas. Two swimmers bobbed in the deep end of the horseshoe-shaped pool to the right, talking quietly. Everything looked so romantic and pristine, with not a detail out of place.

She heard a slam behind her, and turned to see Charlotte, Madeline, and the Twitter Twins climbing from Madeline's SUV. "I always say it's best to plan a prank while trespassing," Lili whispered with a smirk. Her hot-pink bikini poked out from beneath a too-tight white tank top, and she had a purple beach towel tucked under her arm.

Emma ran a hand over the light yellow cover-up she'd found in Sutton's underwear drawer, feeling nervous. The girls were planning the top-secret Lying Game dance tonight, but they were trespassing in the hot springs on the resort property to do so. She would have thought she'd be used to breaking the law by now, but her rule-abiding, good-girl instincts died hard.

My nerves were twisting for a different reason. I knew this place from one of my memories. It was here that my friends dragged me from the springs to the trunk of my car on the night of the snuff film prank, the same night Laurel nearly choked me to death. I'd written that off as a silly prank, but now I wondered. Maybe Laurel had been practicing for the real thing.

Madeline took a swig from an Evian bottle as Gabby and Lili trotted ahead. "I already have so many good ideas," Gabby said over her shoulder.

"We should do overly cliché dance themes," Lili babbled. "For sure we need a punch bowl and a cake that says something like DANCE OFF in pastel icing. And we have to hang *tons* of streamers."

Charlotte, who was wearing a terry-cloth wrap that cinched under her arms, stopped short and grabbed Emma's arm. "Where's Laurel? I thought she was coming with you."

Emma shrugged. "I checked her bedroom before I left, but she wasn't there."

Madeline bristled. "I bet she's with my brother."

Emma figured Madeline was right. She'd been trying to corner Thayer all day to ask how long Laurel had been at the hospital, but every time she'd seen him he was with Laurel.

"Aw," Gabby swooned. "Maybe it's good for Thayer to have a girlfriend."

"Especially if she's one of *us*," Lili added.

Madeline shoved aside a tree branch; Emma ducked as it snapped back toward her face. "Thayer doesn't need a girlfriend right now. He needs to get *better*."

"*Get better?*" Lili repeated. "What do you mean?"

Madeline clapped her mouth closed. Thayer had told Emma that he'd been in rehab, but she was the only person outside of his family who knew.

Unless, of course, he'd told Laurel . . .

"I mean his leg," Madeline said haltingly. "It needs to heal up." And that was that.

"Hot springs, here we come!" Gabby trilled, pushing aside branches. Ahead of them was a clearing of flat red rocks. Three Jacuzzi-sized pools of natural water bubbled invitingly.

I felt a swoop of dread, looking around. Yep, these were the springs all right. That night, I'd gotten pissed at Laurel for wearing a necklace just like my locket, like she was trying to steal my style. She'd claimed later she'd worn it to stage the fight, but clearly she wanted more than my style. She wanted my life.

Madeline pulled her ikat-print caftan over her head and set it on a flat rock near the springs. Charlotte kept her towel on and walked tentatively toward the steaming pool. Emma and the Twitter Twins disrobed, too, leaving their stuff in a pile. Lili dipped her big toe into the water and declared the temperature perfect. As she slid in, she shut her eyes and let out an "*Mmm.*" Emma slipped into the water, too, feeling the warmth envelop her. For a moment, she let her stress float away.

"Okay, time to party-plan," Gabby said, adjusting the gold-tone clasp in the middle of her bikini. "So we're e-inviting everyone who's anyone at Hollier, right?"

"Except the four people we *don't* want," Madeline said. She pushed her hands over the water, creating tiny ripples.

"Maybe we should invite a few cool kids from Wheeler," Lili suggested.

"Like the soccer hotties." Charlotte, who was sitting on the edge, just dipping her legs in, sounded excited.

"Definitely." Emma drummed her fingers on the rocks. "So if we throw the dance at the school, how are we going to break in after hours once the door is locked?"

"Um, the exact same way we did it the last time?" Charlotte said. When Emma gave her a blank look back, she added, "The flamingo and garden gnome prank?"

"Oh, right," Emma said, vaguely recalling seeing a video of this.

"Duct-tape the lock before school's out for the day," Madeline supplied.

"So what are we doing for music?" Emma asked quickly.

Everyone was silent for a moment, thinking. Chirping sounded in the trees. The hot springs were so secluded that every small noise echoed in the still night air.

"I could make a playlist," Lili said.

"I don't think that'll cut it." Emma shook her head. "We need a real DJ. It has to be legit."

"Tank can do it," Charlotte suggested. "He owes me a favor." She shot Emma a knowing look.

I racked my brain for a guy named Tank, but nothing came to mind, and Charlotte didn't elaborate.

"So what if the Devious Four find out about the party and decide to crash?" Emma asked.

Lili twisted her mouth. "We could make everyone show their invites at the door."

"Or we could get a bouncer," Charlotte suggested. "Make things super-classy, even have a velvet rope. I bet the guy who works at Plush would do it for a small fee."

"You know, maybe we *do* want the Devious Four to crash." Madeline's eyes gleamed. "Maybe we want to prank them when they walk through the doors."

"A prank inside a prank!" Charlotte clapped her hands. "I love it!"

Emma bit her lip. She had wanted this prank to be nice, not to embarrass someone. Then again, the Devious Four *had* gotten them into major trouble—and Bethany had asked Ethan out in front of her.

"Speaking of parties," she said, deciding to change the subject. "Have you guys decided what you're wearing to my dad's party on Saturday?"

Lili waded over to Emma and put her arm around her shoulder. "Maybe I'll wear this bikini. Shock a little life into the old fogies."

The girls giggled. Suddenly, a rustle sounded in the brush, and everyone stopped.

Madeline's eyes were wide. "What's that?"

Gabby rose halfway out of the water. "What if it's security?"

"I *so* can't get busted again," Lili whined.

Emma felt goose bumps rise along her arms. The thrashing noise grew louder. Emma made out two figures tearing through the branches. There was a small yelp, and then Thayer and Laurel tumbled out of the bush.

"*God*," Lili murmured, splashing them. "Way to freak us out, idiots."

"Sorry!" Laurel trilled, looking giddy. She took Thayer by the hand. "We were just fooling around." She stared at Emma as she said it. "Sorry we're late."

"Yeah, sorry we're late, Mads," Thayer added, glancing at his sister.

Madeline's expression was stony. "Why didn't you answer my calls?"

Thayer blinked. "I-I didn't hear them, I guess."

Madeline jumped out of the hot spring and snatched Thayer's phone from his pocket. "You don't even have it *on*!" she shrieked.

"I'm *sorry*," Thayer protested, holding up his hands.

Madeline didn't answer. Everyone else was silent, looking around awkwardly. Laurel dropped a canvas tote bag next to a squat rock, pretending not to notice the tension. She slipped out of a white eyelet dress and set a navy blue towel on top of the tote.

Waving his hand in a *whatever* motion, Thayer pulled his black T-shirt over his head. His bare chest was smooth and tan, and his stomach muscles rippled. Emma caught herself looking, then tore her eyes away. It was surprisingly hard *not* to look at Thayer—he was so gorgeous.

"Um, I thought this was a girls-only party," Charlotte said as he edged into the spring.

Thayer raised an eyebrow. "Are you talking about top-secret stuff?"

Emma shrugged. "Kind of, and—"

"Oh, *please*." Laurel rolled her eyes. "Thayer can know. He'll be invited anyway." She cuddled up to him, all the while keeping her gaze on Emma. "Then again, what was that thing you always said, Sutton? *If I told you, then I'd have to kill you?*"

All of a sudden, Emma felt unbearably hot. She didn't like sitting here discussing killing with Laurel, even jokingly. She wasn't sure if she could even be in the same pool with her right now. Not answering, she leapt out of the spring and wrapped her body in a huge beach towel. The cool night air calmed her pulse, and taking deep, even breaths, she wandered down one of the paths, trying to clear her mind.

Emma sank against a boulder and stared at the night sky, wondering just how much longer she could take this. She needed hard evidence against Laurel, something she could actually take to the police.

"Sutton?"

Emma whipped around. Standing before her, his skin glistening and wet, was Thayer. He was out of breath, as though he'd jogged over to her. Emma kept her gaze averted from Thayer's taut stomach. She decided she'd better not look at his arm muscles, either.

"*Thayer!*" Laurel's voice sounded in the distance. "Where did you go?"

"One second," Thayer called, sounding a little annoyed. He looked at Emma, his face full of concern. "Are you okay?" he asked.

"I'm fine," she answered, staring at the ground and trying to marshal her courage. This was her chance to question him. "Um, how about you? Are you having fun with Laurel?"

Thayer's expression tightened. "What do you care?"

Emma's mouth fell open. "Sorry. I was just making conversation."

Thayer's broad shoulders tensed. "I don't get it, Sutton." He shook his head slowly. "I'm trying to move on. But it's . . ." His voice trailed off, swallowed by the night breeze that passed between them. "I can't stand seeing you with Landry," he finally said. "I want to kill that guy."

Oh, Thayer, I whispered, wishing he could hear me. It broke my heart to be so close to him and not be able to explain what I still felt for him, even now. It killed me all over again that Thayer thought my feelings for him were gone.

The cold air chilled Emma's still-wet bathing suit.

"I'm sorry," was the first thing she could think to say. She couldn't imagine how this looked—Sutton had been in love with Thayer before he vanished. He'd been hit by a car on their last night together, and when he came back, she was with someone else. She felt terrible for doing this to him, but then, it wasn't like she could just pick up where Sutton left off with Thayer either.

"And . . . I'm sorry I wasn't the one there for you in the hospital that night," Emma added. "I've wanted to tell you that for so long. I understand why you had to call Laurel, but I still feel like it should've been me . . ."

Thayer scoffed. "Whatever. It's in the past now."

"But I feel terrible about it." Emma heard a splash and a giggle from the hot springs. "Did Laurel at least stay with you?" Emma pressed. "Overnight, I mean. So you didn't have to be alone?"

Thayer let out a laugh, but anger flickered across his features. "Do you really think I'm that much of a wuss? I didn't need Laurel with me to hold my hand."

Emma blinked, needing him to be clear. "So . . . she *didn't* stay with you?"

Thayer shook his head. "She left shortly after she dropped me off. She said she wanted to have a word with you. She was furious, like she wanted to kill you or something. I've never seen her like that before."

Emma tried her hardest not to gasp. It was like the

words had been scripted for Thayer, proving Laurel's guilt. "Oh my God," she whispered.

The words rushed through me, bringing a terrible emptiness. I hadn't realized until that moment how desperately I'd wanted Laurel to be innocent. She was my little sister, the girl I grew up with, who I once considered my best friend. But Thayer's words stripped me of my last shred of hope. She hadn't been with him that night, and she hadn't been with Nisha and the tennis team. I had to face it. Laurel, my *sister*, had murdered me—over a *guy*.

A cough sounded. Emma whirled around and saw a figure standing at the end of the trail. Laurel's light eyes flashed in the darkness. "So *that's* where you are," she said, her voice no longer teasing, but instead flat and cold.

The hair on Emma's arms stood on end. How much had Laurel heard? "W-we were just talking," she stammered.

"Yeah," Thayer said. His glance darted between Emma and Laurel. It was clear he wasn't sure whose side to be on.

Laurel glared at both of them. Then she held up something in the air. Only when a flash went off did Emma realize it was a camera. After that, Laurel whipped around and marched back to the hot springs, her spine ramrod-straight. "Join me when you're ready, Thayer," she called.

Emma and Thayer stared after her, and my heart clenched at the tragic characters in front of me: the boy I loved, the twin I'd never met, and the sister who took both of them away from me.

12

TRACK MEET

The next morning in gym class, Emma and a group of girls walked the perimeter of the track instead of playing handball with the boys. Every girl walked fast enough to appease the gym instructor but slowly enough not to sweat so they wouldn't mess up their makeup during school hours.

Emma tried to listen to the endless chatter about weekend plans, disappointment over how next week's dance had been canceled, and talk about Thayer's return to school, but she couldn't concentrate. She'd barely slept last night, so aware that Laurel was just feet down the hall from her.

Only when she rounded the corner and noticed Garrett climbing into his car in the parking lot did her mind wander for a moment. What was good-boy Garrett doing leaving school property during second period? Even more bizarre, Nisha was getting into the passenger seat. But hadn't Nisha said they weren't hanging out anymore?

I knew Emma's cease-fire with my sworn enemy was too good to be true.

The smell of sunscreen and perfume greeted Emma's nose as a pack of sophomores hustled past. "Hey, Sutton!" Clara called from the middle of the group. The sleeves of her Hollier High tennis T-shirt were rolled up over her tanned shoulders.

"Hey," Emma said absently, moving away from the fence. She didn't want anyone to see her staring at Garrett and Nisha. All she needed was some gossipy underclassmen assuming that she wasn't over Garrett and spreading the news around school.

Suddenly, Emma noticed Ethan sitting on the bleachers across the field and took off in an excited jog. "Hey, stranger," she crooned into his ear, resting her hand on his shoulder. "Is someone cutting class? I thought you had English this period."

Ethan whipped around. When Emma saw his cold expression, she drew back. "I'm kind of busy."

"W-What's wrong?" Emma stammered.

Ethan glanced away, his eyes roving over the track.

"Ethan?" Emma asked softly. But he just sat there, avoiding her gaze.

A cluster of students passed, glancing at Ethan and Emma out of the corners of their eyes. Emma instantly pasted a smile on her face, not wanting them to notice that she and Ethan were fighting.

Finally, Ethan took out his cell phone and turned it toward Emma with a sigh. She stared at a dark, fuzzy picture on the screen. After a moment, she realized it was her and Thayer, standing on the trail, talking. Her heart sank. They were both in their bathing suits. And their arms were almost touching.

Then she realized. Laurel had sent it to him. "Don't you see," she whispered. "She's trying to break us up because she's jealous."

Or she's trying to send you a message, I thought. *She's on to you. She heard what you and Thayer were talking about. Stop while you're ahead.*

Ethan let the phone fall to his side. "Did she Photoshop it? Because you guys look like you're having a romantic tête-à-tête."

"I was asking him about the night Sutton died," Emma said. "You won't believe what I found out."

Suddenly, a metal hurdle clattered on the ground as the

track coach tried to assemble them in an upright position. Emma swallowed hard. They were way too public right here. Anyone could hear them.

"Walk with me?" Emma asked in a small voice. For a moment, Ethan just sat there, like he wasn't going to budge. When he finally slid off the bleacher, Emma let out a sigh of relief.

They began to circle the track, a pack of students sprinting past them. Only when they rounded the corner to a spot behind the field house did Emma yank him off the red asphalt and into the little room that housed the practice mats, javelin poles, and shot puts. When Emma shut the door, only a sliver of light poked through. It would have been romantic if Ethan weren't standing with his arms crossed over his chest.

"Thayer told me that Laurel didn't stay with him all night at the hospital," Emma whispered, her voice sounding tinny and hollow against the low ceiling. "She just dropped him off. And he told me that she was furious at Sutton. He literally said she wanted to kill her."

"Whoa." Ethan let out a low whistle, seemingly forgetting his anger. "That's messed up."

"So how can I prove it before she does something to *me*?" Emma asked. She glanced through the crack in the door, watching as a couple of Hollier kids bounced on the pole vault mat. "I want this over with. This is getting so out of hand. And beyond getting justice for Sutton, do you realize how sick I am of pretending? How I just want to be *me* again? My entire life is on hold. I just realized the other day that I may not be able to go to college."

Ethan's features softened. "I know," he said, wrapping his arms around her.

Emma nuzzled into his shoulder, feeling better. "So you're not mad at me?"

Ethan shrugged. "It's hard to think about you and Thayer together."

"You know I'm into you—and *only* you."

"I know. Really, I do. But I *am* annoyed you didn't invite me to the hot springs. I'd love to know where they are."

"Well, now *I* know where they are." Emma playfully poked his chest. "You and I will go soon—alone."

"Sounds like a date," Ethan murmured.

"You're still planning on coming to my dad's birthday party Saturday night, right?" Emma asked. "*Please* tell me you are. I don't think I can deal with it without you. Especially with Laurel there. It's freaky enough sleeping one room away from her. I've locked the door and the windows every night this week."

Ethan pretended to think about it. "I suppose," he said after a moment. "But only if you're very, very good. And only if you introduce me to this Grandma Mercer."

"You'll love her." Emma rolled her eyes. "But she smells like she bathed in Chanel No. 5. And she'll probably offer you a cigarette."

"Well, then I'll be sure to bring my lighter," Ethan joked. "Oh, and speaking of old ladies, I almost cracked the code on the traffic cameras. The proof that it wasn't you pulling that tree prank will be yours in no time to hand over to Ms. Ambrose."

"*Thank you!*" Emma clutched her hands dramatically. "The Lying Game will *really* love you then. They're already working on another prank for the dance to keep the Devious Four in their place."

Ethan raised an eyebrow. "You're not going to do anything too horrible to those girls, are you? I mean, they're bitches, but I know what you Lying Game girls are capable of."

"*I'm* not a Lying Game girl," Emma reminded him. "And we're only doing what they have coming to them." Then she had an idea. "Maybe the prank-inside-the-prank at the secret dance could be the video footage displayed on a big screen in the gym. That way, the school would know it wasn't the Lying Game who did it. And the Devious Four will finally have to own up to their actions."

It seemed like a good prank to me—effective, but not cruel. I approved.

Ethan nodded. "Works for me. It's time-stop photography, so it'll be like a flip book, not continuous footage."

"Even cooler." Emma leaned against the field house door, suddenly contemplative. "If only there was video footage of who killed Sutton. That would make our lives a whole lot easier, huh?"

Ethan's expression became serious. "Do you really think it's Laurel?"

"Yes, I really do. But that doesn't mean the police will believe me."

"Have you ever searched her room?" Ethan asked.

Emma twisted her mouth. "A few times—at Sutton's birthday party, and I noticed that she'd put Thayer's initials on her calendar the night Sutton died." She raised her head, staring at Ethan's silhouette. Had Laurel known Thayer was coming? Had she followed them to Sabino Canyon and then run Thayer over while aiming for her sister? "But I've never snooped in her drawers or anything. I guess I'll try again."

"Good." Ethan leaned in and kissed her. "You never know. Maybe I'll be attending the next school dance with Emma Paxton."

"Maybe," Emma said, hope creeping into her heart. Ethan took Emma's hand, and they emerged from the field house together.

As the sun blazed down on them like a spotlight, I wondered if Emma would get her happy ending. If after exposing Laurel, she'd live with my family, stay friends with my besties, and go to U of A with Ethan on a full scholarship. But then again, I knew all too well that not everyone got a happily ever after.

13

GRANDMOTHERS KNOW BEST

"Sutton?" a voice called through Sutton's bedroom door Friday night.

Emma jumped off Sutton's bed, where she'd been looking at the *Sutton Mercer Murder Suspects* list that she'd started when she'd first arrived in Tucson. At the top of the page, Laurel's name had been crossed off in thick black ink, but Emma had re-added it at the bottom, just below Thayer's now crossed-out name, and underlined it three times. Just as she slapped the notebook closed and shoved it under her bed, Grandma Mercer poked her head in.

"What's that?" Grandma's eyes narrowed at something on the floor.

Emma followed her gaze. The edge of her notebook peeked out from under Sutton's white bed skirt. "Oh, just doing a little journaling," she muttered dismissively, kicking it farther under the bed.

Grandma leaned in the doorway. As usual, she was impeccably dressed in a tailor-made tweed suit and high heels. Her lipstick was perfect, and her hair didn't move as she walked. There was a slight hint of smoke coming off her clothes. Emma wondered if Mr. Mercer really hadn't noticed yet. "Do you have homework?"

"Not really," Emma said. "I'm pretty much all done."

"Good. That means you can come with me." Grandma offered her hand. "Your father's party is tomorrow, and he's asked me to do some last-minute things." She made a face. "Well, he hasn't *asked* me, per se, but I think some things have been overlooked. For instance, did you know that your mother hasn't designed a lighting scheme?"

Emma opened her mouth, then shut it fast. It seemed to Emma that Mrs. Mercer had planned everything down to the last detail. Mrs. Mercer had made countless calls to the caterer, adjusting and readjusting the menu. They'd hired a salsa band, and she'd been practicing her dance moves at night, stressing because she'd never salsaed in her life. Emma thought it was really sweet that she was putting so much effort into making her husband's party special. But there was no use arguing with Grandma. She seemed like the kind of woman who was going to do things her way, no ifs, ands, or buts.

I wonder if that's where I got *my* stubbornness from. But then I remembered: I was adopted. Grandma wasn't part of my gene pool.

In minutes, Emma had changed into a cotton dress and kitten heels—Grandma deemed that her jeans and T-shirt were "too sloppy" to go to Neiman Marcus in—and she was sitting in the plushy leather passenger seat of Grandma's Cadillac. And minutes after that, they were walking through the Neiman Marcus perfume aisle. Emma's nose twitched from the competing scents.

A memory rippled through me. I was walking through Neiman's with Grandma when I was much younger. A girl at the Estée Lauder counter asked if I wanted a makeover, and Grandma had sat me on the stool. "This will be our little secret," she'd said conspiratorially. Maybe Grandma wasn't so bad, after all.

Grandma peeled off her white leather driving gloves. "Are you excited about your father's party?"

"Sure," Emma said. "If nothing else, it will be nice to see Mom relaxed again."

"Are you bringing a date?" Grandma asked as she paused to sniff a new Dior perfume.

"Yes," Emma said.

"Is it that boy who got in all that trouble?" Grandma asked sharply.

"Thayer? How did you know about him?" Emma said, surprised. Thayer had been Sutton's *secret* boyfriend.

"Your sister told me a few months ago," Grandma said, heading for the elevators. "She said it was obvious. And she said your love for him was—oh, how did she word it? *Obsessive*, maybe. Dangerous."

Suddenly, the smell of the perfumes made Emma a little ill. Why was Laurel saying things to Grandma about Sutton and Thayer?

And it wasn't *my* love for Thayer that was obsessive. It was Laurel's.

"Oh," Emma said quietly. "No. It's someone else. A guy named Ethan Landry."

"Good," Grandma answered. "Because truthfully I think your sister was a little jealous." Then she stopped short in the middle of the scarves department and took Emma's hands. "I know I'm hard on you, dear. And sometimes I probably come off as cold at times. But I just want the best for you. I want you to lead the best life possible, and I get so worried when I hear about you getting in trouble or dating bad boys or not getting the grades I know you can get or having tension with your sister. I just want you to be safe. I just don't want you to end up like . . ." She trailed off, pressing her lips together.

Emma frowned. "Like who?"

An expression Emma couldn't gauge flashed across Grandma's face. It almost looked like fear. But then there was a crash next to them, and she turned. Someone had just knocked a whole rack of scarves over. Salesgirls rushed to the scene and quickly picked them up.

When Grandma turned back to Emma, her face was composed once more. "And to be honest, I'm a little worried about Laurel, too. Is it me, or does she seem . . . *distracted* these days? Almost like there's something weighing on her mind?"

Emma's ears burned. "Um, you could say that," she murmured, more to herself than to Sutton's grandmother.

"Do you know what it is?"

Sweat prickled on the back of Emma's neck and she saw a flash of blond out of the corner of her eye. She turned around and faced the front doors, certain she'd just seen someone jump out of view.

"I don't have a clue," Emma said, swallowing hard.

"Well." Grandma clutched her purse and marched for the escalators. "Whatever it is, it seems like she's up to no good."

No kidding, Emma thought as she followed Grandma up the escalator.

Cool dread washed over me. One thing was for sure. Emma needed to search for evidence in Laurel's room ASAP, and put an end to this charade once and for all.

14

RACKETEERING

Saturday afternoon, Emma stood a foot in front of Laurel's door, her hand poised on the knob. Downstairs, she could hear Mr. and Mrs. Mercer bustling around, making last-minute arrangements for the party, but Laurel was nowhere to be seen. She was probably out with Thayer somewhere.

Twisting the knob, Emma stepped into the bedroom. The smell of Laurel's tuberose perfume greeted her like a rush of heat. Two candles sat on Laurel's desk, along with a cup full of mechanical pencils and a framed photo of five wild mustangs racing across a grassy field. The print was hotel-bland and oddly impersonal in contrast to the collage of photos and tennis ribbons Laurel had tacked up on her wall. Right near her closet was a black-and-white shot of Thayer standing with his arm around Laurel's shoulders in the parking lot of Sabino Canyon. It was slightly askew, and the edge of a different photo poked out from under-neath it. Emma lifted it up to find a photograph of Sutton and Laurel with their arms wrapped around each other in a nearly identical pose to that of Laurel and Thayer.

For a long moment, Emma stood there, studying Laurel's and Sutton's smiling faces. They looked for all the world like best friends.

I squinted hard at it, too, trying to remember when it had been taken. The end of school last year? After a tennis tournament? Maybe even earlier than that—Laurel and I looked so happy. I had no idea what had happened to change that. Maybe we'd grown apart when I'd found cooler friends. Or maybe it really did all come back to Thayer.

The hinges on Laurel's desk squeaked as Emma opened a drawer. Inside was a hot pink eraser in the shape of a heart, rainbow-colored paper clips, and a stapler. Bic pens rolled forward. Scraps of notebook paper lay in piles. Emma picked one up. *Mads*, one of them said. *I need to talk to you about something and it's really important.* Laurel had underlined *really* three times. *Something happened this sum-mer, and I need to get it off my chest. The guilt is eating me alive.*

Laurel. It was dated September sixth, a week after Sutton disappeared.

Emma dropped the note like it was a hot frying pan. Laurel couldn't possibly have considered confessing what she'd done to Madeline, could she? Or was she going to tell Madeline that she'd seen Thayer? Either way Laurel clearly hadn't gone through with it.

Stuffing the note into her back pocket, Emma searched under the bed, under the mattress, and inside the closet. *Nothing.* She was about to retreat when she saw blue athletic tape trailing out from beneath an armchair—the kind of tape she and Laurel used to wrap the handles of their tennis rackets. Emma crouched and saw a racket nestled beneath the cushions. She pulled it out, then turned it over in her hands. The racket's dyed-red strings were bent so badly in the middle, Emma was surprised they hadn't broken. When she touched one of them, some of the red flaked off. It wasn't red dye—it was *blood.*

Emma's fingers trembled at the edge of the racket. The frame was bent as well, as though someone had thrown it hard against something—or someone. Leaning in closer, she saw a long, dark piece of hair twisted along the frame—the same exact color of her own hair. Was that *Sutton's* hair? She fought the urge to be sick. Was Emma holding the murder weapon?

She dropped it fast. Now her fingerprints were on it,

too. She remembered what Ethan had said after she'd told him who she really was: *If you run now, everyone will think you did it.*

Maybe that was exactly what Laurel intended: for Emma to find this. For her to touch it. For the down-and-out twin to be framed.

Creak.

Footsteps sounded on the stairs. Emma shot up just as the door swung open. Mr. Mercer appeared, a startled look on his face. "Sutton?"

"Uh, hi," Emma said, running a hand through her hair, her heart beating hard. She stepped in front of the fallen racket.

Mr. Mercer leaned against the doorjamb, one eyebrow raised. "Does Laurel know you're in here?"

"Um." Emma's mind flew in a zillion directions, trying to find an excuse. "I was just looking for a bracelet Laurel borrowed. I wanted to wear it to your party." She shrugged and lifted the palms of her hands. "But no luck," she said. "I guess she's wearing it today."

Mr. Mercer checked his watch. "Speaking of which, I guess I'd better get ready, too." He patted the door. "I can't be late to my own party, huh?"

Emma forced a smile. As soon as Sutton's father turned away, she kicked the racket back beneath the chair like it was any old tennis racket and not a possible murder weapon. Her stomach churned as images of Laurel bashing in Sutton's head swirled unbidden in her mind.

And they were swirling in my mind, too. I squeezed my eyes shut and tried to call to mind the memory of Laurel pummeling me to death . . . but there was nothing. Just as I was about to give up, an image flashed in front of me: Laurel and me perched on a rocky cliff overlooking Sabino Canyon—the same cliff I'd taken Thayer to. *It's beautiful, isn't it?* I'd asked her. Her light eyes scanned the canyon's walls, and a sly smile appeared on her face. And then, she said, clear as day, *It's the perfect place to disappear.*

15

THE BIRTHDAY SURPRISE

Emma climbed out of Mr. Mercer's car and watched him hand his keys to a blond valet in a red and gold uniform. "Welcome to Loews Ventana Canyon, Mr. Mercer," the valet intoned, gesturing to the hotel behind them.

"Thanks." Mr. Mercer nodded, then strode toward the resort entrance as though he'd been here a hundred times. He probably had—and likely Sutton had, too. But to Emma, this place was all new. Bentleys, high-end Mercedes, and shiny Porsches filled the parking lot. The resort itself was made of clay-colored stone, and it seemed to blend into the cacti-speckled mountain behind it. Two large fire cauldrons flanked the entrance, and Emma

SARA SHEPARD

could see a sleek marble lobby through the grand double doors. *Small-town Girl Goes Five Star*, she headlined in her mind. It made the day spa in Nevada where she'd worked as a towel girl look like a ramshackle car wash.

A prickle of a memory edged my vision. I saw myself and my friends taking a yoga class on the grounds. I could tell it was summer, because all of us were sweating and it was only 7 A.M. At the end of the class, when the instructor had everyone lie down and clear their minds, mine had swarmed with whirling thoughts. I couldn't tell what I'd been worrying about, though. Two-timing Garrett with Thayer? My jealous little sister? Did I know I was weeks—maybe even days—away from my death?

"We're just getting here now," Laurel said into her phone as she and Emma entered the lobby. She was on with Mrs. Mercer, who'd come hours earlier to put the finishing touches on things. Grandma had gone with her and was probably rearranging the table linens and silverware.

Laurel slid her phone back into her clutch and gave Emma a sidelong glance. "You don't seem like you're in much of a partying mood tonight. Cheer up!"

Emma tried not to flinch. Laurel had arrived back at the house mere minutes after Emma had escaped from her room. Emma had watched her go into her bedroom and stand in the middle of the carpet, one finger tapping

136

her lip. Then she'd wheeled around and stared at Emma, who'd quickly turned and hurried into the bathroom as though she hadn't been staring. Did Laurel know she'd been in there? Did she know what Emma had found?

Images of the bloody racket filtered through my mind as I stared at Laurel. Did she feel remorse? How could she pretend everything was okay?

Shrugging off Laurel's comment, Emma followed Mr. Mercer up cobblestone steps and past a crystal fountain filled with orange-and-white goldfish the size of hamsters. She caught her reflection in the floor-to-ceiling mirrors just inside the lobby, barely recognizing herself. She'd chosen an emerald green cocktail dress and gold kitten heels from Sutton's closet. The dress had still had a price tag attached; it had cost over $700. She'd slid into it tentatively, terrified she was going to rip a seam or get deodorant on it.

"*There's* my birthday boy!" a familiar, husky voice rang out. Grandma Mercer, dressed in a black-and-gold ball gown that looked like something a woman of a certain age might wear to the Oscars, floated elegantly through the lobby. She grabbed Mr. Mercer's arm. "Come, come!" she said excitedly, her mouth standing out in bright pink lipstick. "The place looks amazing!"

She shot smiles at Laurel and Emma, and then led them past plush white leather couches that surrounded a fireplace.

Brown-and-black-spotted cowhide rugs covered the rustic wooden floor. Grandma pushed two glass doors open, and they stepped onto a stone patio surrounded by acres of desert overlooking a dark blue man-made pond. The patio was already filled with guests. The men wore a mix of dark suits, linen pants, and crisp button-downs, while women were dressed in chic, jewel-toned cocktail dresses. The sun hovered over the horizon, dyeing the sky cotton-candy pink, and waitresses buzzed amid the crowd with cocktails.

"Kristin has outdone herself," Mr. Mercer said in a she-shouldn't-have sort of voice, but Emma could tell he was extremely pleased.

Grandma's brow furrowed. "I helped, *too*," she said sharply.

Instead of responding to his mother, Mr. Mercer focused on someone across the patio. Emma stood on her tiptoes, and a chill passed through her. It was Thayer Vega, looking effortlessly handsome in slim-cut chinos and a white oxford, his longish hair pushed back off his face. He was talking to his father and nodding adamantly.

Mr. Mercer's face turned pale. He leaned close to Emma and Laurel. "Did one of you invite him?"

Suddenly, Mrs. Mercer sidled up between them. She looked beautiful in a Diane von Furstenberg wrap dress, and diamond studs glinted in her ears. "Is everything okay, sweetie? Isn't this an amazing party?"

Mr. Mercer gave her a look. "What's *he* doing here?"

Sutton's mother followed his gaze, then set her mouth in a line. "Well, I invited the Vegas," Mrs. Mercer said. It was obvious the effort it took to keep her voice calm. "Naturally they'd assume that meant Thayer, too. Now, please, just relax and enjoy yourself. We don't want to make waves."

Mr. Mercer's face turned to stone. "I meant what I said, girls," he said, his dark eyes flashing. "Promise me I can trust you."

Emma threw her hands up in defense. "Of course."

"You can always trust me, Daddy," Laurel added sweetly, tucking a lock of pale blond hair behind her ear.

Almost immediately, Mr. Mercer was swept up by some of his guests, and Emma wandered toward the buffet table, which was stocked with every kind of food imaginable, from sliders to filets mignons, grilled vegetables to complicated-looking soufflés.

After popping a cheese cube in her mouth, Emma looked around to see if any of her friends or Ethan had arrived. Through the crowd, she spotted one of the Mercers' neighbors gesticulating as she entertained a group of women. "And we invited Pastor Wilkins to that book club! Who knew an Oprah's Book Club pick would be so racy!" she trilled. Two little girls sipped Shirley Temples by the bar, pretending they were adults. Then she caught a glimpse of Mr. Chamberlain, Charlotte's father. He stood with his arm around Charlotte's mom, who wore a short leopard-print dress that hugged her flawless figure. Just then, Sutton's father crossed the patio and thumped Mr. Chamberlain hard on the back. Charlotte's dad said something into Mr. Mercer's ear, and Mr. Mercer threw his head back with laughter.

Emma blinked. She hadn't realized those two knew each other. She'd only met Mr. Chamberlain once, the very night she'd arrived in Tucson. He'd greeted her uncomfortably in the Sabino Canyon parking lot, like she'd caught him somewhere he wasn't supposed to be. She sensed something wasn't quite right in the Chamberlain home, but Charlotte had never opened up, and Emma hadn't wanted to pry.

"Sutton?" cried a voice behind her.

Emma swung around and nearly smacked into Charlotte, Madeline, and the Twitter Twins. Each was dressed in a gorgeous cocktail dress. Charlotte's was red, which perfectly accented her peaches-and-cream skin, Madeline's was a vampy purple-black, and the twins wore shiny silver and gold numbers that barely covered their thighs.

"Say *cheese*!" Gabby said, angling her camera to snap a photo. "I'm gonna tweet something about how fun fifty-fifth birthday parties can be—if you have the right attitude." She winked.

Charlotte looped an arm around Emma's shoulders. "Are you having a good time?"

"It's certainly beautiful here," Emma answered, eyeing Sutton's mother and father. They were now standing in front of a big table full of gifts. Mr. Mercer was shaking his head, a please-don't-tell-me-these-are-all-for-me look on his face.

"Where's Laurel?" Madeline scanned the crowd. Before anyone could answer, Madeline shrugged and disappeared, saying something about finding her. By the piqued look on her face, Emma could tell she was afraid Laurel was with her brother.

Gabby sank into one hip, watching Madeline go, too. "Whoa. Hover much? She's tracking him like an ankle bracelet."

"I bet it's because of their dad." Lili gestured across the patio. Mr. Vega was now standing with his wife, picking at a plate full of strawberries dipped in chocolate.

"You know what I heard?" Gabby whispered, her fingers still flying on her iPhone. "Mads's dad is putting all kinds of pressure on Thayer to get caught up in school. *Plus*, he's, like, grounded for life for putting them through hell when he disappeared." She widened her eyes. "Why do you think Thayer vanished, anyway? Mads isn't talking. Do you think he was the leader of a porn ring?"

"No!" Emma exclaimed before she could stop herself.

Charlotte looked curious. "Do *you* know where Thayer was?"

Emma clamped her mouth shut. "Of course not," she said stiffly. "But he wasn't doing *that*."

Then, through the slowly melting ice sculptures, Emma noticed a boy in dark trousers and a light blue button-down shirt appear at the patio door. Her heart soared. "Ethan!" she called, waving him over.

Ethan looked back and forth before locating Emma. A broad grin crossed his face, and he advanced straight for her, not tempted by the waitresses with their trays of food or drinks.

"Hey," he said, looking her up and down. "You look amazing."

Emma kissed him on the cheek, feeling her stomach flip. "You look great, too." She ran her hands through his still-damp hair. His skin smelled like Ivory soap.

Ethan said hello to Charlotte and the Twitter Twins, who greeted him like he was an old friend, then scanned the food spread, which now included a chocolate waterfall and at least ten different types of pies. He let out a low whistle. "This is pretty incredible."

"They went all out," Emma said proudly.

"I didn't know so many people from Hollier would be here," Ethan observed.

It was only then that Emma noticed many of her

classmates peppering the crowd. There were girls from the tennis team and their parents, including Nisha, who looked radiant in a short, white dress, and her dad. A girl from German class was hanging out near the bar with a couple of guys from the tennis team, and a bunch of girls Emma recognized from Sutton's birthday party were giggling near the string quartet. Quite a few of them were staring at Emma and Ethan like they were the new "It" couple.

Emma took a glass of seltzer water from a passing waitress and shrugged. "I think Mrs. Mercer is on the PTA. Maybe she's gotten friendly with other parents over the years."

Ethan looked down. "Yeah, my parents were never really into that sort of thing."

Emma squeezed his arm and gave him a quick kiss before pulling him into a quiet corner.

"I found something in Laurel's room," she said. Then she took a deep breath. "I think it was the murder weapon."

Ethan's eyes widened as Emma told him about the tennis racket. "Did you steal it?"

"No. I was worried she'd notice it was gone. And now it has my fingerprints on it."

Ethan turned toward the crowd for a moment, watching as a waiter passed with a tray full of fruit tortes. "This could be your proof," he went on, his voice urgent.

"I know, but *how*?" Emma urged. "If only we could test that strand of hair, or some of the blood . . . but that would require telling the cops that Sutton is dead." She bit her lip and thought for a moment. "I guess I could write an anonymous note telling the cops everything, and then leave town immediately. That way if they try to pin it on me, I'll already be gone. And I've gotten pretty good at starting over under a new name." Emma let out a rueful laugh.

Ethan looked horrified by the suggestion. "But whoever killed Sutton might come after you for leaving—*or* for announcing to the world that she's dead. And more than that, where would you go, what would you do? Your life is *here*. And it's amazing."

"*Sutton's* life is amazing," Emma corrected. But then her shoulders slumped. "You're right, though. I have no idea what I'd do. I don't have a life anymore. I don't have *anything* anymore."

She turned and looked at the view, taking in the low lights of the wading pool, the tranquil rocks, and the dazzling sunset. Melodic notes from the string quartet filled the air. She allowed herself one moment to actually savor this, to wish that this was *her* life.

Ethan leaned closer. "You have me," he reminded her.

Emma wrapped her arms around him. "Thank goodness for that."

When they pulled apart, Emma felt someone staring at her from across the patio. It was Laurel, who was talking to Madeline and standing *much* closer to Thayer than Mr. Mercer would have liked, though Emma didn't see Mr. Mercer anyway. Laurel was staring menacingly at Emma, and a pang of fear gripped Emma.

Ethan noticed Laurel, too, and pulled Emma tight against him. But even Ethan's protective grasp didn't make her feel better. In fact, being around so many people was beginning to suffocate her. She placed a hand on Ethan's arm. "I need to splash cold water on my face. I'll be right back."

Ethan nodded. "Want me to go with you?"

"It's okay, I just need a minute alone." Then she stepped across the patio and made her way into the foyer of the resort. A cowhide rug splayed out in front of a giant fireplace. Potted orchids sat atop carved-stone tables, and silver-framed pictures of important-looking people dotted the walls.

As she passed through a long hallway, a hushed whisper stopped her in her tracks. Two people were talking just inside one of the dark conference rooms. She would have kept going, but she recognized the raspy smoker's voice immediately.

"Have you seen her again?" Grandma said. Her quiet words seethed with anger.

"Y-yes," a voice answered shakily. Emma clapped a hand over her mouth. It was Sutton's dad.

She peeked around the corner. Mr. Mercer and Sutton's grandmother were standing at the front of the room, near a big, white screen. Sutton's grandmother's face was pinched. The top half of her body arched toward her son.

"What's wrong with you?" Grandma hissed. She looked like she wanted to slap him. "She's toxic for this family. You need to stop this, *now*."

"But—"

"No *buts*. What if Kristin found out?"

Emma blinked hard. *Seeing her. Toxic for this family. What if Kristin found out?*

Was Mr. Mercer having an *affair*?

I couldn't believe it either. My dad didn't seem the type. He acted like such an upstanding citizen, dedicated to his family and his surgery practice. Was everyone in my family keeping horrible secrets?

"Sutton?"

Suddenly, there was a footstep behind Emma. She jumped and turned, knocking into the long stone table against the wall. Thayer's face swam before her eyes, and he whispered her name once more. "Sutton?"

But before Emma could answer, a huge, thin vase on the table wobbled precariously. It tipped as though in slow motion, tumbling to the floor and crashing into a thousand pieces.

In the conference room, Mr. Mercer and Grandma snapped to attention. Their gazes flitted to the vase, then to Emma. Blood drained from Grandma's cheeks. Mr. Mercer's mouth made an O. Emma's eyes locked on Sutton's dad. Running a hand through his hair, he barreled toward her, his eyes blazing.

"Oh my God," Emma squealed, caught. When she turned, Thayer was no longer behind her, but ducking into the nearby men's room. Giving the swinging restroom door no more than a passing glance, she sprinted toward the nearest door, and fled out of the resort.

I was tugged along behind her, away from my father, away from the party, and into the vast desert beyond. But something about the look in my father's eyes, something about Emma running, all of it set wheels turning in my head. All at once, I was tumbling headfirst into another memory.

And it was one I *definitely* didn't want to see.

16

ANOTHER ONE BITES THE DUST

THE NEXT TIME I SEE YOU, YOU'RE DEAD.

What a drama queen, *I think, slipping the phone back into my pocket after pressing* DELETE. *But right on the heels of that thought is a tiny sense of trepidation. Maybe we shouldn't have asked Laurel to take Thayer to the hospital. I know how bad she has it for Thayer. I know how much it would kill her to know that Thayer and I were secretly together. Sure, I'd kind of wanted to rub it in. Sure, I'd kind of wanted to show my sister yet again,* Look! I'm way better than you. *But maybe I'd pushed her too far.*

I look around. It's so dark in the canyon, I can barely see my fingers in front of my face, and my phone's lost service again. I can just make out the road at the top of the incline. The pavement cracks, and pebbles crisscross the path in zigzagging lines. My heart pounds in my throat. I should have been in Nisha's development by now. Am I lost? Did I take a wrong turn? I think about the stories I see on the news about people getting lost up here and never being found. What if that's me? What if I die out here, and coyotes eat my bones?

I'll never go to prom. I'll never get that Marc Jacobs bag I had my eye on. I'll never tell Thayer I love him again. I'll never do anything I wanted to do.

My limbs feel weightless as I whirl in a circle. Desert surrounds me in every direction. I turn to look up at the canyon, hoping I can get my bearings. Rocks soar in a jagged arch, but none of their shapes look familiar. And as I'm swinging around, trying to figure out where the hell I am, I catch sight of a bench halfway up the cliff. Is that . . . a person looking down at me?

But then clouds obscure the moon and I can't make out anything at all. You're losing it, Sutton, *I say to myself, shaking out my hands.* Get a grip. Focus. You're not going to die out here. You're going to find your way out. And just because you and Thayer ran from some freak up here doesn't mean that person is still around. I am Sutton Mercer, and if anyone can find a way out of this, it's me.

An engine groans in the distance. I turn to see headlights blazing over the crest of the road. "Hey!" *I scream, waving my arms. I've never been so thrilled to see a car in my life. I consider hitchhiking—I've done it before, and I really need a ride home. And suddenly, that's where I desperately want to go. Not to Nisha's. Not to Madeline's. But home. All at once, I'm so eager to see my family it almost feels like a hunger pang. I want my mom to make me chicken soup and tell me everything's going to be okay. I want my dad to tuck me in and assure me that the bad guys are never going to get me again.*

I want to tell them I'm sorry for everything I've done lately, too. I've made things so tense at home, ignoring all their rules and being snippy with them at every turn. It's just that with my eighteenth birthday coming up, I want to know about my birth mother—more about where I came from. I could have a whole other family out there that I don't even know about. Maybe even a blood sister or brother. But each time I bring it up, my mom starts crying and my dad gets this thin-lipped expression like somehow I've wounded him to his core. I always get what I want, but my parents aren't telling me anything, so I've been punishing them by partying all night with Mads or sneaking away to meet Thayer when he's back in town.

The approaching car bounces over the rocky earth and the tires kick up a cloud of dust. "Hey!" I cry, waving my arms again. But as the vehicle moves closer, I drop my arms to my sides. Why would a car be driving down this dead-end road? And why do those headlights look familiar? Is it my car? Is the mystery driver back?

Only, the headlights aren't the same shape as mine. Still,

I recognize them from somewhere. I shoot up straight as the car accelerates with a growl, aiming straight at me, covering ground at breakneck speed. It's going to run me over! *I realize, shooting off the path.* Just like someone ran Thayer down.

My mind is suddenly spinning. The next time I see you, you're dead. *Could it be Laurel? Has she lost her mind?*

I whirl around and sprint farther into the desert. The engine responds, roaring louder and veering off the path, too. A voice is calling out, but I can't hear it over the rev of the engine and the pops and bursts of the tires crunching over cacti and sending rocks flying. I'm running as fast as I can, but the car is gaining speed until I can feel its heat and velocity on my heels. The headlights pour golden beams in front of me and I can see my pumping arms in shadow.

"Please!" I scream, twisting around. I try to see who the driver is, but it's too dark—and my eyes are filled with tears. "Please stop!"

The car is just a few feet from me now, about to take me down. All at once, a screeching sound shatters the air. And then, the car stops. I glance over my shoulder just in time to see the window rolling down. They have a gun! *is all I can think, and I zag around a barrel cactus to get away.*

"Sutton!" a voice screams.

I stop. I know that voice. I turn to see my dad hanging out the window. I blink. My heart starts to slow. "D-Dad?" I stammer, slowly walking back to him.

But something's wrong. My dad's face is drawn. The moonlight catches flecks of gray in his dark hair. His eyebrows meet in the middle, and he glares at me like he's disgusted by my very presence. I hardly recognize the way he's looking at me. My dad climbs out of the car, springing forward like an angry rattlesnake. His hand wraps around my arm. Hard.

My mouth falls open. "Daddy," *I whimper, staring down at my wrist where already five red welts are beginning to form.* "Let go. You're hurting me!"

But he doesn't let go, instead continuing to look at me with a rage-filled, searching look, like he's so angry with me he can't even find his voice. "What did you see?" *he finally spits out.*

"N-nothing!"

But my dad squeezes my wrist harder. I stifle a gasp, sharp pain radiating through my arm.

"I know you saw something. Why else would you guys run?" *My father's voice is suddenly so eerily calm that it takes a second for the words to register.*

I know you saw. *My pulse ratchets up as I put the pieces together. This was why Thayer had dragged me away from the overlook and practically pushed me down the trail. He saw my dad doing . . . something—something that scared Thayer. Something that Thayer thought I shouldn't see.*

And that's when I notice there's dust all over him. Desert dust. The same dust that covers me from my race through the canyon. A chill passes through me, and the sound of the footsteps pursuing me and Thayer through the canyon echoes in my head. Someone had followed us. Someone had hit Thayer.

But it seems impossible that it could have been my father chasing us. He loves me. He brought me peanut-butter ice cream when I fell off my bike. He taught me how to serve a tennis ball. He spent hours helping me restore my vintage racing Volvo—the same Volvo that just nearly killed the boy I love.

But the man who's clutching my wrist so hard I fear it might break is someone I don't know at all. Someone capable of hurting me. Someone capable of anything.

"Let me go!" I scream.

My father just wrenches me toward the car. I try to break away from his grip, but he's too strong. My legs kick against the ground, digging in. Adrenaline takes over as I lunge forward and elbow my father in the chest.

"Sutton!" he screams, releasing me.

I turn and bolt. My legs are on fire as I tear across the desert. My feet kick up sand and dirt as I race away from him. My hair flies across my face, and I try to push it away from my eyes. Not that it really matters. I can't see where I'm going, anyway. And it doesn't matter. All I have to do is run and run and run until I've lost him. If I have to run forever, I will.

But from the sound of the engine revving behind me, I realize with sickening dread that I don't have forever. Not anymore. Not if my dad runs me down, just like he ran down Thayer.

17

HIT AND RUN

Dirt crunched beneath Emma's feet as she raced along a desert path. What she wanted, right this second, was to be as far away from Mr. Mercer as possible. She'd seen that look before, in the angry eyes of foster dads. With everything else going on, the last thing she needed was to do battle with him, too.

But maybe my sister's battle *was* with my father. I desperately hoped that I'd misinterpreted the memory I'd just seen. Maybe my dead-girl brain was playing tricks on me. Maybe it was just a dream I was remembering. My dad had never looked at me like that in his life—had never, ever grabbed me or hurt me. *Never.* And yet that night he had.

Soon the sounds of the party faded away, and all Emma could hear was her thudding heartbeat and the sandy gravel under her feet. Slowly, she replayed everything she'd heard between Mr. Mercer and his mother, their cutting argument echoing in her mind. Mr. Mercer was having an affair. Was it serious?

There was a smooth rock ahead, dappled with moonlight. Emma dropped down to sit on it, her limbs aching from running in high heels. As she traced the tiny fissures in the rock's surface, a memory came back to her from her childhood. Occasionally, her mother had had boyfriends, and even though Becky had abandoned Emma when she was five, Emma still remembered a few of them.

Most of the guys worked as truckers, shifty salesmen, or didn't have jobs at all, but there was one guy Becky particularly loved named Joe, and Emma had liked him, too. He'd watched cartoons with her and brought her candy and little toys from the 7-Eleven, where he worked the graveyard shift. He was so much nicer than the other guys Becky dated that Emma began to hope Joe was her father—she was dying for one. But then, one day, Joe stopped coming around, and Becky stopped talking about him. "That jerk cheated on me," Becky snapped when Emma asked where he was. Emma didn't know what Becky meant—in her world, *cheating* meant moving your game piece extra spaces in Candy Land. She'd never even *seen* Becky and Joe play Candy Land together.

Heaving a sigh, Emma slipped off the rock and stretched, knowing she'd have to get back to the party before anyone started asking questions.

A hand clapped down on her shoulder, and Emma jumped. *Laurel.* It had to be. Images of the bloody tennis racket shot through Emma's mind. She spun around, certain she'd see Sutton's sister behind her. But it was Thayer's hazel eyes that blinked back at her.

"Oh!" Emma whispered, wheeling backward.

Thayer's white button-down had come untucked at the waist of his trousers. "Are you okay? Did you . . . hear them?"

"Yeah," she admitted. "I heard everything."

Thayer reached out as if to hug her, then clearly remembering their relationship had changed, awkwardly stuck his hands in his pockets instead. "This was what I was trying to protect you from that night at Sabino," he said. "I saw your dad on the trail with . . . well, someone who wasn't your mom. That's why I tried to keep you away from them—and why I told you to run."

Emma's head snapped up. She'd not been expecting him to say that. "Wait. It was my *dad* on the trail?"

Thayer exhaled loudly. "Yeah. That's why your dad ran after us. He'd realized I'd seen him," he went on, sounding

tormented. "I'm sorry I didn't tell you. I was going to . . .
but then I was in the hospital, and then I went back to
rehab, and then you stopped returning my emails."

My head was spinning right along with Emma's. That
desert dust I'd seen on my father. I'd been *right*. It *was*
him we were running from. Him and some awful, home-
wrecking woman. That was why he demanded to know
what I saw. But had he come after me to bribe me to stay
quiet—or shut me up for good?

"I haven't told Laurel," Thayer went on, pausing to
wipe sweat from his brow. "And I don't think you should
either."

Emma stared at him, feeling like her head was stuffed
with cotton. "Why not?"

He bit his lip. "She isn't as strong as you are. I just
found out she was a complete mess after she took me to
the hospital."

"Well, she was really angry at me," Emma pointed out.
"You said you thought she wanted to kill me."

Thayer shook his head. "Yeah, but I was at physical
therapy this morning, and a nurse asked me how my girlfriend was. I thought she meant you at first, but she was
talking about 'the blond girl, the girl who stayed the night
I was hurt.' Apparently, even though I told her to go,
Laurel stayed in the waiting room, sobbing." Thayer took
a breath, then ran his hand through his hair. "The nurse

said she was so hysterical that they gave her a sedative and kept her in the hospital overnight for observation. They didn't want her driving in that condition."

Emma blinked as Thayer's words started to sink in. She laced her hands behind her neck, trying to get her bearings. "Hold on. Laurel was in the hospital all night . . . and it was my *dad* at the canyon that night," she repeated.

"Yeah," Thayer said softly.

An owl hooted in the distance. A cloud passed over the moon. Emma looked at him. "Did my dad ever say anything about that night to you? Any kind of explanation for why he was there?"

Thayer's eyes narrowed, and he made a small, incredulous noise at the back of his throat. "I'd say him running me down with your car was a pretty clear indication that he never wanted me mentioning that night again."

Emma bolted upright, her limbs on fire. "*He* hit you?"

This isn't happening, I thought. *This cannot be happening. What I saw was no dream.* Every last gritty, horrifying detail was real.

Thayer looked at Emma and shrugged. "Who else could it be? Your dad was chasing after us. And whoever hit me was driving *your* car. He has your keys, right?"

I had dropped my keys beside my car that night, but my dad definitely had a spare set, too.

Emma's mind reeled, and suddenly everything she had

thought to be true was turned on its head, and another picture began to click into place. So Laurel *didn't* do it. But someone else was there the night Sutton died. Someone who had a motive to keep Sutton quiet. Mr. Mercer. And then something else occurred to her. What if Mr. Mercer wasn't just trying to protect his affair? What if Sutton had threatened to tell the police that he'd run down Thayer? What if he'd killed her to shut her up?

But Mr. Mercer was Sutton's *father*. Could it really be true?

Emma sank back onto the rock, placed her head in her hands, then, unexpectedly, burst into sobs. Maybe it was the stress of holding it together for so long, but suddenly, tears were streaming down her face fast and furious.

I wished I could cry, too. From shock. From numbness. From the unfairness of it all. But as hard as I tried, I couldn't muster a single tear.

"Is this why my dad wanted Laurel and me to stay away from you?" she asked, her voice muffled through her fingers. "Because you'd tell us he's cheating?" *And because you'd tell me he'd hit you with his car and then killed the twin I didn't even know I'd had?* she added silently.

"I don't know," Thayer said softly. He took a small step toward Emma. "But maybe." And then he sat down, pulled her close, and hugged her tight. "You'll be fine. I promise," he whispered ever so softly into her ear.

At first, Emma's body was stiff, but Thayer felt so good against her that she began to relax. She needed someone to hug her right now. She needed someone to tell her it was going to be okay. Emma allowed herself to cry for a few minutes until the tears died out and the sobs were just little hiccups.

I stared at the two of them, feeling an uneasiness that had nothing to do with what I'd just learned about my dad. Thayer was hugging a girl who looked just like me . . . but *wasn't* me, and there was nothing I could do to stop it.

After a moment, Emma broke free from Thayer, feeling awkward. "I should . . . I need to be alone," she mumbled, brushing the tears from her face. It was true, but she needed to be away from him, too. It wasn't fair to Ethan to be taking comfort in another boy's arms—especially when that boy was Thayer.

Thayer stared after her, his eyes soft in the moonlight. "You know I'm always here for you, Sutton."

"Thank you," Emma said faintly, then moved down the path toward the hotel, taking even breaths as she processed everything Thayer had just told her. Mr. Mercer had killed his own daughter because she'd known what he did.

But I *hadn't* known it was him—not until he showed up in his own car. It had been so dark that night, and I hadn't seen the driver. And I hadn't seen him with his mistress because Thayer had protected me from the truth. He'd done what my dad was supposed to do—take care of me and keep me out of harm's way. How could my father live with himself? Didn't he *love* me? But then the memory I'd just seen flared in my head again. As much as I wanted to erase it, it only got darker, inkier. That car heading for me. Those harsh words, *Get in the car, Sutton!* That hand around my wrist, those strong muscles dragging me in the dirt.

Even though no one could hear me, I opened my mouth and wailed. My killer was my father.

18

WATCH YOUR BACK

That night Emma lay in Sutton's bed, wide awake. She'd fled from the party after her discussion with Thayer, not wanting to face Mr. Mercer. She'd sent Sutton's friends quick texts before she left, saying she didn't feel well, but she knew it probably looked crazy. Once she'd gotten back to the Mercers', she'd had a long call with Ethan, discussing everything she'd learned. He'd wanted to come over immediately and only backed down when Emma promised him she'd call him first thing tomorrow; she couldn't risk Mr. Mercer realizing that Ethan knew about him, too.

Then she'd locked herself in her bedroom, pushed Sutton's dresser in front of the door, and thrown the covers over her head. Mrs. Mercer had knocked on Emma's door an hour ago and asked if she was okay, but Emma had pretended to be sleeping. *It was probably something she ate,* she'd heard Sutton's mom whisper in the hall. *Or something she drank,* Grandma Mercer groaned. Emma didn't hear Mr. Mercer at all.

She knew the sick excuse wouldn't hold for long— she'd have to face the family sometime. Mr. Mercer knew she'd heard him. But did he know that she'd put the pieces together? And what was Mr. Mercer waiting for—why hadn't he killed her already? He had to know how much snooping she'd done. Would he make it look like she'd died in an accident? That way, both Emma and Sutton would be gone in one fell swoop.

I'd also wondered if my murderer was biding his time, figuring out the best way to kill Emma so that it seemed like an accident—a car wreck, overdose, nasty fall. My dad was a doctor and had access to all kinds of drugs. Was he planning to poison Emma in her sleep, then play the role of grieving father for the rest of the world?

The white curtains billowed like ghosts. Sutton's cavernous closet was ajar, revealing neatly hung dresses and blouses. Her computer flashed a rotating screen saver of her best friends. Now that Emma had uploaded new photos, pictures of both her and Sutton flashed across the screen. There was one with Sutton in her Hollier tennis uniform. The next one captured Emma and Charlotte at La Encantada, posing in crazy outfits in the Neiman's dressing room. The only difference in the twins' smiling faces was the tiny scar on Emma's chin, which Emma had gotten from falling off the Hamburglar at a McDonald's PlayPlace when she was little.

Emma sat straight up. Mr. Mercer had pointed out that scar the very first morning she'd eaten breakfast with the family. Maybe it was some kind of warning, that the smallest difference could blow her secret if she wasn't careful.

She flopped back in bed, filled with dread and fear and heavy sadness. Mr. Mercer seemed so sweet and caring, like the kind of man who'd do anything for his daughters, which made it all the more heartbreaking that he'd done something so terrible.

I squeezed my eyes shut, disgusted at the whole idea of it. Of everything that'd happened since my death, this was the hardest to process. I felt like I was drowning every time I thought of the ways my father had let me down. How could he cheat on my mother? He had to know it would destroy our family. And how could he kill me? How could my father squeeze the life out of me, his daughter? Maybe he'd never loved me. Maybe I was just some adopted daughter he'd never really wanted in the first place.

With sleep nowhere in sight, Emma rolled over and

pulled out her Sutton investigation notebook from under the bed and opened it to an empty page. *Mr. Mercer,* she wrote at the top. It pained her to even pen such a thing.

Then she leaned back to think. Had he known about Emma all along? Had Becky mentioned that Sutton was a twin when she put her up for adoption? Had he put that video of Sutton getting strangled on the Internet, hoping Emma would see it and come forward? Emma had always thought it was some sick coincidence that Travis, her then–foster brother, had found the snuff video that led Emma to Sutton the very night Sutton died. But Mr. Mercer must have gone through Laurel's Lying Game videos and found one that would get someone's attention. And then he'd hijacked Sutton's Facebook account and written back to Emma. Sutton kept herself auto-logged in. It all would have been so easy.

Then Emma thought again about that first morning she'd eaten breakfast with the Mercers. Mr. Mercer had disappeared from the house in the middle of coffee, saying he was grabbing the paper. He had time to affix the *Sutton's dead* note to Laurel's car. He was friends with Mr. Chamberlain, and if Sutton and her friends knew the Chamberlains' alarm code, it was definitely possible that Mr. Mercer did as well. For all Emma knew, the Mercers housesat for the Chamberlains when they went on vacation. Emma wasn't sure how he could have gotten into the school auditorium unnoticed to drop the light on her, but Sutton's father was agile—he went for runs every morning before work and sometimes hiked on the weekends. He was probably capable of a lot.

A creak sounded in the hallway, and panic welled inside Emma's chest. What if that was Sutton's dad? There was another loud creak, definitely a footstep. Emma stifled a small sob. It had been terrifying living under the same roof as Laurel when Emma thought she'd killed Sutton. But Mr. Mercer was twice her size. Emma wouldn't stand a chance.

The doorknob started to turn. Heart in her throat, Emma waited for the door to open and bang into the oak bureau, but then Drake let out a yelping bark, and the doorknob turned back into place.

Emma's pulse was still racing as the footsteps retreated along the hall. She stared up at the ceiling. Moonlight illuminated a miniscule web of cracks that fanned out from the light fixture overhead. Emma counted them over and over, wondering if she'd ever be able to sleep again.

19

ONE BIG UNHAPPY FAMILY

Emma stayed like that for the rest of the night, with the covers pulled up to her chin. Every clang of a pipe or swish of air inside a vent made her heart race. When she'd heard Mr. Mercer's alarm sound at 6 A.M., followed by the creak of the stairs as he walked down in his running shoes, she'd leapt to the window to watch him jog down the street casually and easily. Like he wasn't a murderer. Like he hadn't tried to come into Emma's room last night to possibly kill her, too.

By ten, Emma desperately had to use the bathroom. Reluctantly she climbed from bed and stumbled down the hall, locking the door behind her. She got in the shower, letting the sound of rushing water drown out her sobs. When she finally collected herself, she turned off the tap and used her palm to clear the steam from the mirror. She stared at her reflection and for a second pretended it was Sutton's periwinkle eyes staring back. "I need you, Sutton," she whispered. She knew it was crazy to talk to her dead twin, but she *felt* a little crazy right now. "Tell me what to do. Tell me how to solve your murder. Tell me how to incriminate him."

I stared back, wishing I could download my memory onto a DVD and play it for Officer Quinlan. But I couldn't. All I could do was watch and hope my sister didn't end up like me.

After Emma dressed, she opened the bedroom door to find Laurel standing with her hand poised to knock. "*There* you are," she said. "Ready for breakfast, or are you still too sick?"

Emma stared blearily at Sutton's sister. Out of habit, her muscles tensed, and she tightened her jaw, but then she realized—Laurel wasn't a suspect anymore, for *real*. All of a sudden, she wanted to throw her arms around Laurel simply for not killing Sutton.

But then she registered Laurel's question. Breakfast meant facing Mr. Mercer. "Um, I'm still feeling pretty bad," she mumbled.

"Oh, come on." Laurel linked her arm around Emma's

elbow. "Dad's famous pancakes will fix you right up."

Before Emma could protest, Laurel dragged her down the stairs and into the kitchen. When Emma saw Mr. Mercer's tall, straight back at the stove, pouring pancake batter into a frying pan, she froze. *Murderous Father Plays the Part of Doting Family Man,* she thought, picturing a grainy, black-and-white photograph of Mr. Mercer holding a spatula and grinning maniacally into the camera.

I watched my father, too, wishing I could grab him from behind and shake him hard. "How *could* you?!" I screamed at his back. "I trusted you! I *loved* you!" But as usual, my voice instantly evaporated, like I'd yelled into an airless tunnel.

Mr. Mercer turned and stared at Emma. His lips spasmed slightly, as though the effort of holding back his anger in front of Laurel was too much for him. "Oh. Sutton. You're awake." He awkwardly scratched a spot by his nose. "Feeling better?"

Emma cast her eyes down, feeling her cheeks burn. "Uh-huh," she mumbled.

Laurel slumped into her regular breakfast seat. "You missed the best part of Dad's party, Sutton—the cake. It was ah-*may*-zing. Then again, you seem to be ditching all kinds of parties these days, including your own." She rolled her eyes.

"It was a nasty case of food poisoning," Emma

mumbled, clutching her stomach for effect. "In fact, I should probably go upstairs and lie down some more. I'm still feeling dizzy."

"Nonsense. A little food in your stomach will do you good," a sharp voice said to Emma's left. She looked over and saw Grandma at the table, a mug of coffee before her. Her eyes were cold, and she looked Emma up and down with pursed lips. "Funny, you don't *look* sick." Her gaze shifted to Mr. Mercer. "Does she?"

Mr. Mercer flinched, dropping the ladle into the batter bowl. Emma's heart was pounding so hard she was sure everyone could hear it.

"What do you think poisoned you?" Laurel asked, looking a little worried. "I hope I don't get sick, too."

Emma shifted her weight, suddenly not remembering a single morsel of food that had been served at the party. "Uh, a hot dog, maybe," she blurted, thinking of the time she'd gotten food poisoning from a hot dog she'd bought at a Vegas street stand.

Grandma gave Emma a pointed look. "Hmm. I thought the food was delicious. Are you sure it wasn't something else that . . . *upset* your stomach?"

"She said it was the food, Mom," Mr. Mercer snapped. "Just drop it."

Grandma's wrinkled lips flattened into a frown, but she stayed quiet.

Laurel swiveled back and forth, staring at all of them. "Uh, does someone want to let me in on the joke?"

No one answered. Emma shrank against the wall, wishing Grandma would keep her mouth shut. She was playing with fire—and she didn't even know the half of it.

Just then, Mrs. Mercer swept into the room, all sunshine and happiness. "Everyone's up!" she trilled. "And we're all having pancakes! How lovely!" She glided over to Mr. Mercer at the stove. "And how's the birthday boy? Did you enjoy your party last night?"

Mr. Mercer swallowed hard and mumbled a less-than-enthusiastic yes.

Mrs. Mercer poked his side. "You'd better be happier about it than that! I thought it was a resounding success! Didn't you, Gloria?"

She looked at Grandma. Grandma Mercer's gaze was still on Emma. "I think it had its good moments and its bad moments," she said in a pinched voice.

Mrs. Mercer paused and stared from Grandma to her husband to Emma. "Did I miss something?" she asked tentatively.

"That's what *I* want to know," Laurel said. "They're all acting really weird."

"We're acting fine," Mr. Mercer said quickly, flopping several pancakes on the plate so forcefully that one nearly flipped onto the floor. He carried the plate over and set it on the table. "Voilà. Enjoy."

Mrs. Mercer reached for a pancake, the chipper expression returning to her face. "So, girls, I found out last night from Mr. Banerjee that the school dance was canceled because of some kind of vandalism," Mrs. Mercer said. "What happened?"

Laurel grabbed the syrup, which was in a striped ceramic jug. "Oh, it was just a stupid thing. Some freshman girls did it, but because they won't fess up the dance is off." She poured the syrup onto her stack of pancakes. "I heard that it's really canceled, though, because the teachers wanted to use the money they set aside for the dance to go to some off-site conference at a spa in Sedona."

"Really?" Mrs. Mercer said, her brow crinkling. "Well, I'll be sure to bring that up at the next PTA meeting."

Laurel took a big bite of her pancake and washed it down with orange juice. "Sutton and I will be home late that night, though. The tennis team is having a get-together after practice."

She was lying, of course. But the Mercer parents weren't likely to go along with their daughters breaking into the school gym to throw a dance. "It'll be fun to do some team bonding off the court," Laurel chirped. "Don't you agree, Sutton?"

Emma glanced up from her plate of pancakes. "Um, yeah," she mumbled. "Really fun."

"And the get-together was Nisha's idea," Laurel went on, meeting eyes with Emma.

Mrs. Mercer's eyes lit up. She had Nisha on a pedestal like some teenage version of Mother Teresa. "That girl is always thinking about what's best for the team," she murmured.

Grandma Mercer stared at Emma. "Just like you, Sutton. Remember last year, when you made those team T-shirts? Your father told me about how clever your wording was. What was it again?"

Emma looked up and felt four pairs of eyes on her. Mrs. Mercer, Laurel, and Grandma just looked inquisitive, interested. But Mr. Mercer's gaze was cold and threatening. She could practically hear his thoughts: *Keep playing along. Keep your mouth shut.*

Emma jumped up abruptly, nearly upending the jug of syrup. She couldn't stand another second of this. "Um, can I be excused?"

Mrs. Mercer looked surprised. "Are you still not feeling well?"

Emma shook her head, careful to avoid eye contact with everyone.

Mrs. Mercer let out a note of concern. "Oh, you poor thing!" she said, following Emma out of the room. "Is there anything I can do for you? Get you some ginger ale? Bring you up some of your favorite DVDs?"

Emma stared at Mrs. Mercer. Her face was so kind, open and giving. All of a sudden, she felt a swell of sympathy for her. *Your husband is cheating on you*, she wanted to say. *And I think he killed your daughter.*

"Thanks," she murmured, standing on her tiptoes and wrapping her arms around Sutton's mom. When she pulled away, Mrs. Mercer looked surprised, but also touched.

Sadness settled in my chest. It was, I realized, exactly what I'd yearned for the last night I was alive, when I was lost in the canyon. All I'd wanted was the safety of my mom and dad.

Little had I known that my dad was the one I should fear the most.

∽ 20 ∾

WHERE IT ALL BEGAN

Sunday evening, Emma pulled into the dusty parking lot of Sabino Canyon. As she cut the engine, she looked at Sutton's Volvo with disgust. Normally, Sutton's car calmed her—there was something so special about the shiny chrome, the buttery leather, even the effort she had to put into turning the steering wheel since automatic steering hadn't been invented when this car was built. But now, all she could think of was Mr. Mercer behind the wheel, using this car to mow down Thayer. The police had fingerprinted the car when it was impounded last week. At the time, Emma had thought nothing of it when

Quinlan said the only prints in the car belonged to Sutton and her father. But she knew better now.

The lot was empty and dark, the only light from the half moon shining overhead. Emma locked the Volvo behind her and made her way across the gravel to the bench where she'd sat on her very first night in Tucson. The world had felt so full of promise then. She'd thought she'd meet the twin she never knew she had and maybe, just maybe, become part of Sutton's family. How ironic that her new life had begun in the exact same place her sister's life had ended—and that she'd only become part of Sutton's family because Mr. Mercer killed his adoptive daughter.

All day, Sutton's dad had continued to be sharp with Emma, and so had Grandma. The two of them had been snippy with each other, too, making everyone else in the family uncomfortable. By the time Grandma had left, she and Mr. Mercer were barely speaking. Grandma had given Emma a big hug before she got in her car, squeezing her tight. Then she'd leaned in and whispered, "Don't go getting into any trouble."

Emma hadn't known what to make of Sutton's grandmother's warning. Did Grandma *know* what her son had done to Sutton? But that seemed inconceivable. Grandma might have been tough as nails and as prickly as a cactus, but she wasn't a killer.

Emma kept picturing Mr. Mercer hitting Thayer with Sutton's car, then abandoning it for the cops to find. Had he disposed of it before or after he'd killed Sutton? How exactly had he killed Sutton? And where had he stashed her body?

I was wondering all the same things. And I kept racking my brain for clues that my dad had been having an affair. Had I ever seen him skulking around, acting weird? I remember having a flicker of us not being so close anymore—could that be why? Maybe I'd sensed something was off before Thayer and I had come upon my dad and the woman at Sabino Canyon. Maybe I'd even confronted my dad, and then kept my distance. But frustratingly, I couldn't put my finger on a specific memory.

Footsteps crunched toward the bench, but Emma didn't flinch. She'd texted Ethan on her way over, asking if he'd meet her here. His and Nisha's houses were just a few blocks away. He sat down next to her, slipped his hand into hers, and tipped his face skyward.

"How are you holding up?" he asked softly.

"Not great," Emma admitted.

"You look exhausted." Ethan shut his eyes. "I'm guessing you didn't sleep at all?"

Emma shook her head. "How can I? He's right down the hall. I think he tried to come into my room last night," she said, fiddling with the cuff of her jacket.

Ethan's jaw dropped. "But he didn't?"

"No. Drake stopped him."

For a while they were just silent. A brisk wind whipped through the canyon, brushing Emma's hair off her shoulders. She glanced at the myriad of trails leading up into the mountain range. It was so beautiful in daylight, but now it looked like a hulking mass, ready to swallow whole anyone who dared hike it.

"I can't believe it all happened here. I can't believe that Mr. Mercer hit Thayer, then went after his daughter *right here*," Emma whispered, looking around cautiously, like Mr. Mercer might leap out at them at any moment. But aside from a roadrunner darting across the lot, they were alone. "I need real proof. Only . . . how?"

Ethan swallowed, looking sick to his stomach. "There has to be some hard evidence somewhere," he said. "Research he did on you before contacting you. Or maybe someone else knows about what he did—like this woman he's having an affair with. Maybe he wrote an incriminating email. Or maybe he plans to see this woman again, and we could follow them."

Emma nodded. "She was there that night in the canyon. What if she helped him cover it up? If I could figure out who this woman is, maybe I could get her to corroborate the story." Then she frowned. "But how do I find out that stuff?"

Ethan thought for a moment. "Does your dad use Gmail?"

Emma shrugged. "I think so."

"He might have a calendar on there." Ethan asked for Sutton's cell phone, logged into her email, and then looked at the shared calendars she had with the rest of the Mercer family. "Here," he said, showing her the screen. "Your dad shares his work schedule with your mom and you. It looks like he's out of the office Thursday afternoon for a conference."

"So?" Emma asked, peering at the screen. "He really *could* be going to a conference. Not meeting with a woman."

"Yeah, but either way, he's *not* in his office—that's a perfect opportunity for *you* to sneak in. You don't think he'd keep that kind of information at home, do you?"

Emma paused. She'd never thought about that. "I guess someone having an affair would want to hide it, wouldn't they?" she murmured. "Will you come with me?" The idea of breaking into Mr. Mercer's office freaked her out.

Ethan gave the phone back to Emma, looking chagrined. "I can't. I have to take my mom to another doctor's appointment that afternoon."

Emma bit her lip, not wanting to complain. "Okay. But can I call you after?"

Ethan squeezed her hand. "Of course."

"I wish it was sooner. I don't know how to make it until Thursday," Emma said softly.

"You can do it, Emma. You're so close."

Emma closed her eyes. "After my mom left, I wished every night that she would come home and pick me up. She used to love treasure hunts," Emma said, remembering the little notes Becky would leave under her pillow or in the egg tray in the fridge. "I thought if I could just figure out the clues, I'd find her again. We'd move into our very own house, get a golden retriever, and be a real family. We'd be happy. But I've lived with dozens of families now, and not one of them seems happy."

A cloud shifted over the moon, momentarily plunging them into complete darkness. "My family certainly isn't happy," Ethan muttered. "But I don't think it's the way it has to be. At some point, you get to choose who you're with." He cleared his throat awkwardly. "Like we're choosing to be together."

Despite her stress and exhaustion, Emma couldn't help but smile. "Well let's choose to be together, here, for a little while longer. I'm not ready to go home yet."

Ethan leaned back into the bench and put his arm around her shoulder, settling in. "We can stay here as long as you want."

★ ★ ★

Hours later, Emma lay in bed, glancing every so often at Sutton's bureau, which she'd once again pushed in front of the door. To stay calm, she'd started a *Cute Couple Stuff I Want to Do with Ethan* list, which included making each other iPod playlists of meaningful songs, and a *Most Romantic Things Ethan Has Ever Said to Me* list, which featured Ethan telling Emma that he would protect her from Sutton's killer, no matter what.

"Come out and play," a voice suddenly sang.

Emma sat up straight in bed, looking wildly around.

"Come out . . ." the voice sang again. But it wasn't Mr. Mercer. And it wasn't coming from the hall, either.

Emma went to Sutton's window and drew back the curtain. And there in the front lawn, standing underneath the large oak tree, was a woman with stringy dark hair and a round face. Emma's jaw dropped. It was her mother, Becky.

She was so much paler than Emma remembered, her skin a ghostly white against the night sky. Tattered rope bracelets crossed both of Becky's wrists. Her worn jeans were rolled up at the bottom to expose her long, thin bare feet. Her faded red T-shirt hugged her slim shoulders and flared out at her stomach. The words on it were blurry, but the shirt suddenly felt achingly familiar—Emma knew she'd seen it before.

So had I. I couldn't place it, but I knew the T-shirt

like it was one of my own—maybe I'd seen it in one of Emma's dreams?

"Mom?" Emma called. She leaned forward and squinted, trying to get a better glimpse of her mother, but Becky kept her eyes cast down at the wet earth. Emma could barely make out her face in the darkness.

"Hold on, Mom. I'm coming!" Emma said, shimmying out Sutton's window, grabbing onto a tree branch, and swinging to the ground. Rainwater soaked her feet and ankles, dampening her nightgown. As soon as Becky saw her, she took a step backward, like a scared animal.

"No, Mom, *wait*," Emma called, pushing through the thick night air. "I want to talk to you."

"I don't want to talk. I want to play," Becky said in a childish voice.

"Please?" Emma said, reaching out. "I need you to help me. I need you to make sense of all this."

Becky lifted her gaze to meet Emma's. Her eyes were an icy, ghostly blue. "I'm so sorry," she said. "For everything I've done. For disappointing you." She swiped a dark lock of hair away from her eyes, leaving a streak of mud like war paint across her forehead. "For leaving you."

Emma reached her arms out. "Please hug me," she begged.

But Becky just stepped back. "I'm watching you. I've been watching you this whole time, Sutton."

Emma blinked. "I'm not Sutton."

Becky tilted her chin as though she didn't quite believe what Emma told her. "What do you mean?"

Emma tried to rest her hands on Becky's arms, but they were too slippery—as though a slick, icy substance covered her skin. "I'm Emma," she said. "Don't you remember?"

Becky shook her head vehemently. "You're in *Sutton's* house," she said, inching farther away from Emma. "You have to be Sutton!"

She suddenly looked furious. She stepped forward and grabbed for Emma's wrists, missing them. "Tell me the truth! Tell me who you are!" She swiped again, this time slashing Emma's skin with her long nails. But as soon as she touched Emma, Becky disintegrated into a heap of ash. Someone laughed in the distance. It sounded like Mr. Mercer's throaty, baritone chuckle.

Emma woke with a start, cold sweat soaking Sutton's pajamas. She was back in Sutton's bed, nowhere near the windows. The glowing numbers on Sutton's alarm clock read 2:03 A.M. She wrapped the covers around her and tried to catch her breath. She rubbed her eyes again and again, but she still couldn't completely rid her mind of the dream images that flitted behind them. Becky had seemed so close, like she'd been lurking around the Mercers' house, just waiting for a glimpse of her daughter.

It was the same wish she always had—that Becky was

somehow keeping tabs on her and still cared about her life—especially during times of stress. But it was foolish. Becky didn't care about her twins. She was reckless and self-absorbed and capricious. She had abandoned both of her girls without looking back.

Now one of her daughters was dead. And the other was living with her killer.

21

WANDERING MINDS

"Okay, major breakthrough for our party on Friday!" Charlotte trilled as she flopped into a seat next to Emma in the library on Monday afternoon. "I talked to the guy at Plush, and he can be our bouncer. And I got this awesome deal on hors d'oeuvres from this caterer my mom uses. Isn't that amazing?"

Emma tried to muster a smile, though she was surprised at how loudly Charlotte was talking. Not that the librarian on duty, a college-age boy who had big headphones over his ears, seemed to care. Study halls at Hollier, Emma noticed, involved very little studying. Even the kids who were reading were looking at dog-eared copies of *Vogue* and *Sports Illustrated*.

"I got a lot done, too!" Gabby exclaimed, pulling up a chair. "Lili and I sent out invites over the weekend, and everyone seems really into it. Some people seemed a little nervous, since it's on school property, but I have it on good authority that Ambrose and all the administrators are going to be in Sedona at that conference."

"We're totally in the clear," Lili affirmed. "And we told everyone to park far away so the cars won't attract attention."

Charlotte grinned at Emma. "Our own dance, sponsored by the Lying Game!"

"Mm–hmm," Emma said vaguely. She reached over to pull Sutton's phone out of her bag, but the whole thing tipped over instead. Books spilled onto the carpet. Her water bottle rolled under the next table. Instantly, two girls sprang up and scooped her books into their arms. A guy she didn't recognize saved her bottle and gathered Sutton's makeup. Everything was returned neatly to her purse without Emma having to move a muscle.

"Typical," Gabby said, rolling her eyes. "We're back on top, now that everyone knows about the secret dance and wants an invite."

"Is something distracting you, Sutton?" Charlotte asked, looking concerned.

"Of course not," Emma said quickly, though she knew it sounded like a lie. She'd been thinking about

Mr. Mercer all day, turning the case over and over in her head.

"So I've invited the usual people, plus a bunch of kids from the newspaper, student council, the fashion club, the crew team, and yearbook," Gabby reported, smoothing down her plaid pleated skirt. "Lili sent invites to juniors, sophomores, and a few freshmen. We're trying to keep it exclusive so we don't get busted. The Devious Four are going to be so pissed, though—obviously, they weren't on the list."

"But we'll make it easy for them to crash, right?" Charlotte asked.

"Uh-huh." Lili tapped away on her phone. "And then we'll nail them."

Charlotte looked at Emma. "How's Ethan coming on that video footage? I love your idea about projecting it onto the gym wall."

"I think he's getting pretty close," Emma said. Actually, she wasn't sure how Ethan was doing with the footage—it hadn't exactly been at the top of her priority list. They'd spent the rest of last night in silence, looking up at the stars, and holding hands until Emma had to drag herself back to the Mercers'.

Emma shook her head. Mr. Mercer was certainly a good actor—he'd behaved like he had no idea where Sutton's car was, going along with Emma's story that it was at Madeline's. He'd played the loving, if occasionally awkward, father to a T. Was it possible he was used to lying about things, covering up secrets? Was it possible he had a criminal past?

She thought about what Grandma Mercer had said about Mr. Mercer living in California for years before abruptly moving to Tucson shortly after they adopted Sutton. Perhaps he had a criminal record there. People didn't become murderers out of nowhere, after all. Waiting until Thursday to search Mr. Mercer's office felt so far off. Maybe if she looked into Mr. Mercer's past, she could find some previous incidents that would help prove that Mr. Mercer had a violent streak.

A violent streak. I couldn't stomach it. Had I ever seen my dad be violent before that night? If only I could just *remember.*

"Earth to Sutton," Gabby said, waving her hands in front of Emma's face. "Did you even hear what I said?"

When Emma looked up, Gabby, Lili, and Charlotte were staring at her quizzically. She wondered how long she hadn't been paying attention. She brushed a lock of hair behind her shoulder and straightened up. "Um, totally," she fudged.

The shrill blare of the bell startled them. Everyone rose from their seats and headed for the door, chattering excitedly, as this was the last period of the day. Buses idled on the curb outside. A line of cars had already begun to form at the exit.

Madeline was waiting in the hall, her coat on. Charlotte quickly filled them in on the plan to coordinate outfits.

Madeline's eyes lit up. "Ooh, shopping! Want to go tomorrow when you guys are done with practice?"

Everyone nodded. Charlotte turned to Emma. "I guess we'll fill Laurel in at practice."

Madeline made a face. "I don't know if we should include her—she seems to be a little too busy hanging out with my brother to help us plan. I think someone might need her Lying Game privileges revoked."

"That might be a tad dramatic, Mads," Charlotte said in a soothing tone. She shifted her weight. "Right, Sutton?"

Emma nodded quickly. Now that Laurel wasn't a suspect, she saw the situation for what it was: a girl who had a massive crush on her hot best friend. Laurel wanted to spend as much time as possible with Thayer in order to win him over—or maybe to keep him away from her older sister.

Madeline shrugged, then spun on her heel and marched in the opposite direction. Lili and Gabby followed, still texting. Charlotte touched Emma's arm and steered her down the hall the other way. "Is something bothering you?" she asked softly.

Emma took out her hair tie and let her long hair spill over

her shoulders. "I'm fine," she said. "Just a little stressed out lately, I guess." Even if she couldn't tell Charlotte what was really wrong, it felt good to admit that she was struggling.

"Can I ask you something?" Charlotte said as they skirted around a bunch of girls looking at something on their phones. Emma overheard the words *invite* and *secret dance*. "You weren't really sick with food poisoning at your dad's party, were you?"

Emma's head shot up. She opened her mouth, but no sound came out.

"Someone said they saw you outside with Thayer," Charlotte said out of the corner of her mouth.

Heat rose to Emma's cheeks as she started up the stairs. "They said you were holding hands," Charlotte went on. "And that you looked upset."

Emma glanced over her shoulder. "Who said that?"

Charlotte stopped on the landing, letting kids pass by. She lowered her eyes. "Actually, it was me—I saw you. But I'm worried. Is everything okay? What were you guys talking about?"

Emma glanced at Charlotte. For just a split second, she considered spilling everything. But how? *Actually, Char, I'm not really Sutton, but her twin. And I think her dad killed her, and I think he's forcing me to be her until he gets around to killing me, too. And, oh yeah, I think he hit Thayer with Sutton's car. No biggie.*

"We were just talking about old times," she said stiffly.

"Are you thinking about getting back together? What about Ethan?"

"Ethan and I are fine," Emma said. "Like I said, we were just discussing something that happened a long time ago. It's not a big deal, I swear. Stop worrying, okay?"

"You just haven't been acting like yourself," Charlotte protested. "It's like aliens have come down and swapped out the Sutton I thought I knew with someone else."

Emma stared at her. It was chilling how close Charlotte had come to the truth. But then she took a deep breath, wrapped her arms around Charlotte's shoulders, and gave her a big hug. "I assure you, I haven't been abducted by aliens," she said. "Now let's just go to practice and forget about all of this."

"If you're sure," Charlotte said, looking a little more relaxed.

And then they headed out the door, taking a short-cut to the locker rooms. Halfway there, Charlotte stopped and said she forgot her calculus book in her locker—she needed to go back. "I'll catch up with you," she said, spinning around.

Emma continued toward the locker room, her head in a fog. Exhaust billowed from the buses. Someone blew a horn on the street. She had to pass a back parking lot to get to the locker rooms, but it was usually quiet this time of day, reserved for teachers and faculty. But today, something caught her eye. Someone was standing just outside a black SUV, staring at her. When she realized who it was, she stopped, her blood running cold.

It was my dad. And he was looking at Emma the same way he'd looked at me the night I died.

22

PLAY ALONG

Pretend you didn't see him, Emma thought instantly. She put her head down and shuffled toward the locker room, her heart pounding hard. But then she heard a metallic sound of a hand slapping a car door. "Sutton!" Mr. Mercer's voice called.

Emma stopped and peeked at him. "Oh, hey, Dad!" she said pleasantly, as if just noticing him for the first time.

Mr. Mercer didn't look amused. He walked around to the other side and opened the passenger door. "Get in."

Emma's fingers shook. "Thanks, but I drove here," she said, holding up her car keys and trying to sound normal.

"I can get home on my own. And anyway, I have tennis practice now."

"Get. In. The. Car," Mr. Mercer said sternly. Then, seemingly realizing he was in a school parking lot, his lips formed a small smile, probably for the sake of anyone watching. "We need to talk, okay?" he said in a gentler voice.

The whole scene felt chillingly familiar. *Don't do it, Emma*, I urged.

Emma didn't budge from the square of pavement where she stood. She glanced around, hoping—praying—that someone would come around the corner and see this. Amazingly, there was no one. If only she could reach into her pocket and text Charlotte for help, but Mr. Mercer would see. And anyway, what would Charlotte say when she got here?

"Sutton?" Mr. Mercer said warningly.

Not sure what else to do, Emma walked over to the car and climbed inside. The SUV was chilly, the AC on full blast. The cold metal of the seat belt buckle felt like ice against her thigh.

Sutton's dad shut his door and rested his hands on top of the steering wheel. He drummed his fingers on the thick leather, seemingly collecting his thoughts. Emma shrunk down in the seat and focused on the chipped beige polish on her fingernails, trying to remain calm. *You're going to be all right*, she told herself. *We're in a public place. He can't do anything to you here.*

Yeah, until they drive away, I thought. *And then what?*

Finally, Mr. Mercer let out a sigh and looked at her. "You and I have needed to talk for a long time now." His words came out slowly, like he was measuring each one. "We might as well get it out in the open."

Mr. Mercer took a long breath. "That night in the canyon changed all of our lives. I didn't plan for it to happen that way. . . ." His voice trailed off. "But I was doing it for you." His expression was beseeching. "I thought it would make things better. I thought it was what you wanted."

The air in the car seemed to plummet another ten degrees. Emma could barely keep her jaw from dropping. Was he talking about her life in Nevada, as a foster child? Was he intimating that he'd killed her twin to rescue her from foster care?

Jesus. The horror I'd previously felt had now multiplied exponentially. Was my dad really that insane? Did he hate me *that* much?

Anger burned in Emma's chest. "How could you think it would make things better?" she squeaked. Her fingers curled around the door handle.

But Mr. Mercer grabbed her arm before she could get away. When Emma turned, his eyes were blazing again. "Look. We have a good thing going here. Don't you think? Do you really want to ruin everything? For your mother, for yourself?"

Emma stared at him, but no words came out.

"I didn't think so," Mr. Mercer said. He placed his hands on Emma's shoulders, pressing her into the seat. "Keep playing along. Everything will be okay."

Emma was too afraid to even breathe. His words mirrored the ones used in the first note the killer left her: *Sutton's dead. Tell no one. Keep playing along, or you're next.*

He'd confirmed everything she suspected to be true. Rage suddenly flowed through her. He'd done this to Sutton—to her. He'd brought her here to cover up his heinous crime. Then he'd threatened her, again and again, to keep quiet. And all for . . . what? Some woman? Keeping up family appearances?

My shock and sadness and horror turned to fury, too. My own father had killed me. There was no question, and there was no good reason. Parents were supposed to *love*, not kill. They were supposed to protect their children, not throw them away like they were a pair of last year's boot-cut jeans. I wasn't *dispensable*. I wasn't *nothing*.

Emma whipped around and grabbed the handle again. Mercifully, the door wasn't locked, and she was too quick for Mr. Mercer. All at once, she was on the curb and running across the parking lot.

"Sutton!" Mr. Mercer roared. But Emma kept going.

She never felt so relieved to see the girls' locker room; Mr. Mercer couldn't follow her in there. She went straight into the bathroom and locked the stall door behind her.

"Oh my God," she whispered into her hands. What was she supposed to do now? How was she going to outsmart Mr. Mercer and get the evidence she needed without him killing her? How much time did she have left?

I didn't know the answers either. And for me, I was still stuck on what my dad had just said. His words played over and over in my mind like a broken record. *Keep playing along.* Like this was a *game.*

I rested my fingers around Emma's as I'd only done once before—the night she was trapped in the cave with Lili and we both thought everything was over. That time, I was comforting her. But this time was different.

This time, I was the one who needed my sister.

23

THE RATTLESNAKE IN THE ROOM

Tuesday after practice, Emma pulled into the parking lot of La Encantada, the luxe shopping mall in the Tucson hills. She threw the car into park just as her phone buzzed in her lap.

ANY LUCK GOOGLING MR. MERCER? Ethan asked.

NO, NOTHING. HIS NAME IS TOO COMMON, Emma typed back.

HMM. I'LL TRY LOOKING, TOO, Ethan said.

THX. YOU ARE THE BEST, Emma responded.

Emma had been a wreck after her conversation with Mr. Mercer, but luckily he hadn't come home from the hospital until almost midnight. In addition to googling him and Mrs.

Mercer, she'd checked the home study to see if there was anything there about their past. But aside from some old tax forms, she hadn't seen any evidence of their life in California.

"Uh, hel*lo*?" Laurel's face appeared in the window. She'd driven herself, but Emma had followed her into the parking lot. "What are you doing, zombie?"

Emma jumped, slid Sutton's phone into her purse, and pulled the keys from the ignition. By the time she climbed out, Laurel was already walking impatiently toward the shops. "It's past six," Laurel called over her shoulder. "What do you want to bet Gabby and Lili found all the best dresses already?"

"They can't wear every single amazing dress to the party," Emma pointed out. The plan was to hit Anthropologie, BCBG, J. Crew, and a bunch of other boutiques in the shopping plaza.

Laurel stepped onto the escalator and gripped the hand-rail hard.

"So are you excited for the party?" Emma asked.

"Uh-huh," Laurel said stiffly.

"Looking forward to really sticking it to the Devious Four?"

Laurel grunted and glanced away.

Emma sighed loudly. She had enough on her plate without Laurel's mercurial moods. "Okay, Laurel. What did I do this time?"

Laurel swung around and rode the escalator up backward, resting her hands on the arm rails. "Fine," she spat. "Dad said you were snooping in my room. *Again*."

Emma blinked, barely remembering searching Laurel's room. Now that Laurel wasn't a suspect, it was like her mind had erased all of the Laurel-themed sleuthing.

Laurel set her mouth in a line. "Were you looking for love letters between Thayer and me? Well, I have a surprise for you, Sutton. Something that will make you very happy." She brushed a honey-blond lock behind her shoulder. "Thayer's not into me that way." Her voice trembled a tiny bit.

"Oh, Laurel, I'm sorry," Emma said softly, stepping off the escalators. She reached out for Laurel's arm, but Laurel pulled away.

"He told me last night that he's still into *you*," Laurel said, her voice low, like it pained her to say the words. "I just don't get it. If you guys are still into each other, why did you break up?"

Emma blinked. Two sets of shoppers passed before she could speak again. "I'm not into him, Laurel. I swear."

Laurel rolled her eyes. "Yeah, right. I heard about you two having a secret powwow the night of Dad's party."

A muscle in Emma's jaw tensed. "Did Charlotte tell you?"

Laurel's eyes widened. "So it *is* true?"

Emma sighed. The meaty smell of the steak house

down at the end of the esplanade was beginning to give her a headache. "It's true, but it's not what you think. We were just talking. There's nothing between us any-more. I really, really like Ethan." Emma placed her hand on Laurel's arm. "Look, I'm sorry about Thayer. And I'm sorry about going into your room without asking," she said. "I promise I won't do it again. I was just looking for those red leather sandals you borrowed for Homecoming. I was thinking of wearing them to Dad's party."

Laurel glanced at her. "With that green dress you had on? Are you kidding?"

"I thought it would make a statement." Emma grinned.

"Yeah, you would have looked like a Christmas tree," Laurel said with a laugh, and just like that, the tension lifted.

As they started toward BCBG, where the girls were meeting first, Emma realized she needed to clear some-thing up. She looked at Laurel. "So what was up with that disgusting tennis racket under your chair?"

Laurel blinked, looking like she didn't know what Emma was talking about. Then, a light appeared in her eyes. "Oh my God. I totally forgot about that. I used it to kill a rattlesnake in the backyard last week. It was awful."

"Ew!" Emma said, relieved to have Laurel off her suspect list for good.

Then Laurel sighed. "And actually, it was sort of awful of Dad to tell on you."

Emma swallowed hard. It was dangerous to involve Laurel at all, but she knew Mr. Mercer better than anyone. Perhaps she'd noticed something. "Yeah. He's been acting kind of strange recently, don't you think?" she said.

"Maybe a little," Laurel said with a frown. "But I think he just doesn't like Thayer."

Before Emma could press for more, Laurel's phone blasted a Rihanna song, scaring some of the nearby shoppers. She fumbled for her phone inside her crocodile-embossed handbag, then pressed the speaker button. "Hey, Dad," she singsonged.

"Hi, darling," Mr. Mercer said. His voice echoed off the hard surfaces in the mall. The hair on Emma's arms stood on end.

"Sutton and I are both here," Laurel said. "What's up?"

"Sutton's there, too?" Suddenly, Mr. Mercer sounded guarded. "Oh."

Emma curled her toes inside Sutton's four-inch wedges.

"Uh, what time are you girls coming home tonight?" Mr. Mercer asked.

Laurel glanced at Emma and shrugged. "We're shopping right now. I guess I'll be home after that. I don't know about Sutton, though."

Emma's throat felt like it was closing. "Actually I'm not

coming home," she said, making a snap decision. "I'm sleeping at Charlotte's. Please let Mom know." Charlotte would
definitely go for it, and the only way Emma was going to
feel safe was if she was anywhere but Sutton's house.

"Fine." Mr. Mercer's voice was stern. "Tell Mr.
Chamberlain I said hello. And remember our conversation,
all right, Sutton?"

Laurel shot Emma a questioning look, but Emma
leaned over, plucked Laurel's phone from her hands, and
hit the END button before any more could be said. Then
she composed her features, trying to act like this was just
another one of Sutton Mercer's bitchy little moods. Laurel
just stared, slack-jawed.

"Whoa," Laurel finally said. "What did you do this
time to get on Dad's bad side?"

You have no idea, I thought.

"And what conversation was he talking about? Did he
catch you with Thayer at the party, too?"

"No," Emma said tightly as BCBG came into sight.

Luckily, the Twitter Twins were standing in front
of the store display, picking on the mannequins. "Who
would accessorize with those hideous belts?" Gabby was
saying of the one on the right.

Lili wrinkled her nose at the other mannequin, which
was holding an oversized quilted bag. "And why do they
have to make the models so freakishly thin?"

"Ladies," Laurel said.

The Twitter Twins spun around and gave Laurel and Emma big smiles. "Three more days 'til the secret dance!" Gabby trilled.

"Wait till Mads tells you what happened," Lili said, chomping on her gum.

As if on cue, Madeline and Charlotte appeared at the escalators. The girls strode over, and everyone air-kissed.

Gabby nudged Madeline. "Come on. Tell them about your run-in with the Devious Four."

Madeline rolled her eyes. "I wish you wouldn't call them that. It gives them too much credit. Anyway, those stupid girls cornered me after school today and begged me to invite them to the party." She tucked a strand of inky black hair behind her ear and crossed her arms over her chest.

"And?" Laurel looked excited. "You said no, right?"

"Of course I said no," Madeline said. "But you should have seen them. They practically got on their knees and begged."

"Good. That means they'll definitely try to crash," Charlotte said decisively. "And once Ethan gets that footage, they'll be the stars of their very own little movie."

"I can't wait to see their faces," Gabby said. "The footage was such a great idea, Sutton."

Emma smiled. For once, she was proud of a Lying

Game idea. It wasn't particularly mean, just fair. And she liked that it involved Ethan, too.

"No one messes with us. Right?" Lili said. She nudged Emma.

"Right," Emma said, forcing a smile.

But we both knew that wasn't true. Someone had done a lot worse than mess with us. Someone had killed me, and my friends had no idea.

24

MANO A MANO

The lunch bell rang on Wednesday, and Emma opened Sutton's locker and stared at its contents. Since she'd taken over Sutton's life, she'd made some rearrangements, taking down the little locker-sized mirror and replacing it with a picture of Johnny Depp, her longtime crush, and removing the snarky magnet that said I'M THE QUEEN OF THE WORLD, AND YOU'RE MY BITCHES and swapping it with a magnet of Stewie from *Family Guy*. It was one thing for Sutton to be a queen bee; she didn't need to announce it to the whole school via her locker.

As Emma grabbed her coat, her phone buzzed in her purse. Her heart almost stopped when she pulled it out and saw that it was Mr. Mercer. She let the call ring through, and a moment later she got a voicemail alert. With shaking fingers, she pressed LISTEN.

"Laurel said you're not coming home again. I'll cover for you for one more night," Mr. Mercer barked into her ear. "But if you're not back tomorrow . . ." His voice trailed off and the message ended with a click.

Emma gazed at the phone. She almost wished he had just said his threat outright so she could bring it to the police. But he was too smart for that. At least she didn't have to deal with him tonight. She was staying at Madeline's—Charlotte's parents were hosting a dinner party that night for some of Mr. Chamberlain's coworkers—but it looked like tomorrow, she'd have no choice but to go back to the Mercers'.

Exhaustion settled around her like a heavy cloak. If she could have curled up inside the locker, she would have. Luckily she was having lunch with Ethan. She needed some quality one-on-one time with the only person she could let her guard down with. He'd been such a rock these past few days especially—he'd called her every night before bed, and had even brought her flowers at Charlotte's. Mrs. Chamberlain had proclaimed him a keeper.

Emma leaned against her locker for a second and shut her eyes. When she opened them again, she found herself staring at Thayer. She jumped, startled.

"Whoa!" Thayer said, holding up his hands. "Just me!"

Emma's mouth wobbled into a smile. "H-hey," she said, taking in Thayer's hazel eyes and gleaming skin. She hadn't seen him since Sutton's father's party, though he'd texted Sutton's phone a few times. The moment they'd shared had felt a little too intimate for her, and she'd wanted to keep her distance.

Thayer moved a little closer, leaning his hip against the bank of lockers. "I just wanted to check in to see how you're holding up about . . . everything," he said softly.

"I'm . . ." Suddenly, Emma's gaze locked on someone behind Thayer. Sutton's ex, Garrett, had spied both of them, and was barreling toward them fast. His jaw was clenched, and his eyes were narrowed into little slits.

Thayer turned, too, and gave Garrett a cautious wave. Garrett just stared at him. "I wouldn't waste your time talking to Sutton, man. She's over you. She has a new boyfriend now. Or haven't you heard?"

"Garrett!" Emma exclaimed.

Thayer rolled his eyes, ignoring him. "Get lost, dude."

Garrett let out an ugly snort. "Oh, I forgot," he said sarcastically. "You don't have much respect for relationships, do you?"

He stared at Thayer. Thayer stared back. For a long moment, neither boy blinked. "Back off," Thayer said through his teeth.

"Or what? You'll sleep with my girlfriend? Oh wait, you already have. Because you're both sluts."

Thayer's face turned bright red. Then his fist met Garrett's face, and Garrett was clutching his jaw. The very next second, Garrett was grabbing Thayer's shoulders and shaking hard. Thayer tried to remain upright, but his knees buckled and he stumbled on his bad leg.

"Guys, stop!" Emma shrieked, yanking the back of Thayer's T-shirt. "Please!"

Garrett took another swing at Thayer, but Thayer ducked and circled his arms around Garrett's waist. Both boys let out guttural groans, and suddenly they were on the floor, rolling around.

"Stop!" Emma shrieked again.

I watched in horror . . . but also in awe. I wasn't sure if two boys had ever fought over me before, and it was kind of flattering.

"Fight!" yelled a scrawny guy in a flannel shirt. Instantly, Hollier students materialized from out of nowhere, gawking at the boys on the ground. Members of the marching band streamed from the auditorium to watch, and kids swarmed from classrooms, forming an amoeba-like cluster around Garrett and Thayer. Half the crowd held up their cell phones to capture the action.

Now the boys were on their feet again. Thayer lunged at Garrett, but a soccer player Emma recognized intervened and yanked Garrett out of the fray. "Stop it, man," he growled into Garrett's ear. "Fighting will get you kicked off the team."

Garrett struggled against him, his eyes blazing and his chest heaving hard. "You're an asshole," he hissed at Thayer.

"So are you," Thayer spat, standing in the middle of the circle. His nose was dripping blood.

The crowd began to break up as quickly as it had formed. Emma rushed to Thayer and touched his shoulder. "Are you okay?"

"That guy is crazy," Thayer rasped, catching his breath. He ran a hand over his jaw and winced.

"You shouldn't have provoked him!" Emma cried.

Thayer rotated his shoulder gently, then met her gaze. "It's one thing for him to say things about me. But I can't stand him insulting you."

A warm feeling swelled in Emma's stomach, and she felt herself blush. It was kind of touching that Thayer was so chivalrous, standing up for her like that. Even sort of . . . *romantic.*

I was touched, too. Especially because he was standing up for *me*, not my sister.

Someone cleared his throat behind her. Emma turned and saw Ethan nudging through the remnants of the crowd, looking worried and confused. Emma sank into him, relieved Ethan couldn't read her thoughts. "Hey," she murmured.

"What's going on?" he asked. "I heard there was a fight and you were in the middle of it."

Emma shook her head, glancing from Ethan to Thayer, then back to Ethan again. It felt weird to talk about what the fight was about. "It's over," she said simply. "And I'm fine. Thayer was . . . protecting my honor."

Ethan glanced at Thayer for a long moment, then he stuck out his hand. "Well, in that case, thanks, man."

Thayer shook it. "Anytime."

Then Ethan put his arm around Emma's shoulders. "Want to get out of here? We could do lunch off campus or something."

"Okay," Emma said quietly. She glanced over her shoulder once more to say bye to Thayer and make sure he was okay. But he was gone.

Fifteen minutes later, Ethan pulled his rattling Honda Civic into a parking lot surrounded by ivy-covered trellises and beautiful rose gardens. A quaint restaurant called Le Garçon stood a few feet away in an old Victorian mansion that looked like an overgrown gingerbread house. It was incongruous to see such architecture in adobe-filled, Southwestern-style Tucson, which made it all the more exotic.

"After the week you've had, I thought you could use a little break," Ethan said, leading her into the restaurant. It was cool inside, and smelled like fresh flowers. When Emma's eyes adjusted to the light, she could see a few tables covered with white linens. Oak beams crisscrossed the ceiling, and tiny vases held light pink roses alongside white Christmas lights. The back doors were flung open to the enormous garden, and a harpist played soft, tinkling notes in the corner.

"Whoa," Emma said, watching as the waiter passed with trays of rich-looking food. "This seems really fancy, Ethan. And expensive." She glanced at him worriedly. "Do you want me to pay?"

"Of course not." Ethan made a face. "I got this covered."

Emma took his hand as a maître d' led them to a table.

I was surprised and impressed by Ethan's choice, too. It was exactly the kind of date I would've planned—secluded enough to be romantic, but populated with the right kind of crowd.

They sat down and spread their napkins across their laps. A waiter came by and poured each of them a glass of water, which Emma drank thirstily. Ethan watched her, his chin resting in his hands. "You're beautiful, you know that?"

"Stop." Emma ducked her head.

"It's true," Ethan insisted. "But you also look tired. Have you been able to sleep at all?"

"Only a little," Emma admitted quietly. She scanned the room. Aside from a couple of well-dressed women a few tables over, who gave Emma a quick glance and then looked away, the bustling restaurant didn't seem to notice them. "I just want tomorrow to get here already so I can search Mr. Mercer's office. I'm sick of biding my time. I want this over with."

Ethan reached across the table and took her hands. "Of course. But let's try not to think about it, okay? You need a break—you *deserve* a little while off the case."

His voice was gentle but firm, and Emma forced herself to loosen her shoulders. "Okay," she whispered.

At the next table over, a woman in a tight black dress and a man in a skinny tie studied the wine list. A few people were sitting at the bar, laughing pleasantly. The vibe was understated, but classy. Emma had a feeling her sister would have loved it here.

I smiled. She was right.

"Oh!" Ethan said with a broad grin. "I meant to tell you, I finally got into the traffic cam system! You were right, it was the Devious Four."

"That's amazing!" Emma exclaimed, leaning over the table to give him a quick kiss. "The girls will be so happy!"

"Yeah, I'll just splice together the footage and email you guys the file," Ethan said, his cheeks a little flushed.

"Perfect."

A waiter set a basket of assorted rolls on the table. "Would the lovely young couple like to hear the specials?" he asked, jutting one hip forward and smoothing a hand over his carrot-colored hair. "The tuna tartare is out of this world. And don't get me started on the braised lamb chops with mint sauce." He made an orgasmic face.

Emma giggled. "That sounds delicious. I'll have that," she said.

"Great choice!" the waiter trilled. "And for you, sir?"

"I'll have the shrimp cocktail," Ethan said, breaking off a piece of rye bread and popping it into his mouth. "And, um, the steak. Medium rare."

"Medium *rawr!*" the waiter faux-growled, curling his hand like a lion, then sauntered off.

For a moment, Emma kept her eyes on her lap, but when she saw Ethan's mouth wobbling into a grin, she burst into laughter. They exchanged a glance, and both started giggling harder. "*Rawr!*" Ethan imitated.

"Great choice! Too bad he doesn't work at the cafeteria at Hollier," Emma joked. "Can you imagine? 'Uh, I'll have the French bread pizza.' '*Great choice!*'" she said, moving her hips from side to side flamboyantly.

"Or at a prison lunch line." Ethan hunched his

shoulders and spoke in a thuggish voice. "Yo, man, I'll have the meat loaf slop and a side of yesterday's green beans."

"*Great choice!*" Emma crowed in refrain, snorting with giggles. "Or what if he were the telephone operator at a sketchy Chinese restaurant?"

Ethan held up his hand to his ear, imitating a telephone. "Uh, hi, I'll have General Tso's chicken?"

Emma winced. "*Great choice!*" She giggled.

They were laughing so hard now that everyone in the restaurant was staring at them. Emma knew they were being completely immature and inappropriate, but she didn't care. It felt so good to laugh. It felt good, too, to share such a fun moment with Ethan. This was why she was with Ethan: They shared the same sense of humor. They understood each other. And they had so much fun together.

"I love seeing this side of you," Ethan said when the giggles died down. "It reminds me that no matter how well you pull off Sutton, you're uniquely yourself."

Emma nodded. "We're alike . . . and not alike. Kind of two sides of the same coin. Sometimes I think I'm losing myself to her."

"You aren't," Ethan insisted. "You'll always stay you."

Emma stared at the glass bottles of alcohol behind the bar. "I can't wait to become me again," she said softly. "Mr. Mercer said that this situation is so much better than what I had before. But I miss being me. I want my life back. My own choices."

"I know," Ethan said. "I can't wait for you to be Emma, too." Then he took her hands. "But you have to admit that becoming Sutton has had *some* benefits?" He squeezed her palms. "Like meeting me."

"Like meeting you," Emma said, returning his gaze. They leaned forward and kissed lightly.

I turned away, feeling like I was eavesdropping on something personal. Emma's words rang in my ears. I wanted her to go back to being herself, I really did. But it raised another point that I didn't think of very often. When Emma put my dad behind bars, what would happen to me? Was I tethered to her because I had unfinished business? Or was it some horrible karmic screw-you for all the terrible things I did while I was alive?

Emma had everything to gain by getting justice for me. She would move on to the next stage of her life as Emma Paxton. Would I move on, too? Or would I be left with nothing at all?

25

MIDNIGHT SNACK

After practice and a long, hot shower, Emma knocked on the Vegas' front door. She heard footsteps and a moment later, Madeline opened the door, put a finger to her lips, and ushered her inside.

Despite their light footsteps, Mr. Vega appeared from the kitchen, carrying a tumbler of amber-colored liquid, presumably Scotch. His cold, steely eyes canvassed Madeline as though looking for a flaw. Then he stared at Emma. "Isn't it a little late for a get-together, girls? It's a school night."

Madeline cleared her throat nervously. "Daddy, we have a really big physics test tomorrow, and we're going to be studying well into the night. Can Sutton *please* stay over? We won't make a peep—I promise."

Mr. Vega swirled his drink, looking like he didn't quite believe them. Even in repose, he seemed coiled and anxious, ready to strike. Emma held her breath, forcing herself not to look at Madeline's arms and legs. The bruises were expertly masked by sleeves and yoga pants, but Emma knew they were there. And she knew who'd put them there. She couldn't believe this place was her alternative to the Mercers'.

He wasn't on my suspect list, but he was a criminal. Now that I knew what Mr. Vega was doing—to Mads *and* Thayer—I got a chill whenever I saw him. It explained why Mads got so nervous when she was around him and why she fought to be perfect. She probably thought that if she could just get it right, he wouldn't be able to find anything to criticize.

"Fine," Mr. Vega finally said, holding their gazes for a disconcerting beat too long. "But keep it down. Your mother is already asleep."

Emma wondered if Mrs. Vega had ever tried to stop her husband from hurting her kids, or if she was too scared of him to intervene.

In seconds, they'd dropped their stuff in Madeline's room. Pictures of ballet dancers spotted Madeline's walls. Framed magazine spreads hung next to photographs of her and Thayer. Porcelain figurines were arranged in a circle on her spotless dresser. She wondered if Madeline's uber-strict father made her clean it every morning or if this was Madeline's way of exerting control where she could.

Madeline shoved a bunch of pillows off her lilac-covered duvet and plopped down on her queen-sized bed. Hugging a pillow, she eyed Emma suspiciously. "You know, I'm all for the impromptu sleepover and every-thing, but why have you been avoiding going home all week? Did you have a fight with Laurel or something? Are your parents getting on your nerves?"

Emma eyed Madeline, glad she had given her a plausible out. "Laurel's been really bitchy lately. I just needed a break from the constant fighting."

"About Thayer?" Madeline asked sharply.

Emma stared at her feet. "Kind of."

Madeline's shoulders stiffened. "If you're sneaking around with him behind my back, Sutton, I swear I'll—"

"I'm not," Emma assured her. "I mean, we've talked a couple of times, but it's not like that." She sat down on the bed next to Madeline. "I've got a good thing going with Ethan. He makes me really happy."

Madeline flashed Emma a genuine smile. "Ethan does seem pretty great. Who knew the brooding poet would be such a good guy? I'm happy for you two."

"Thanks," Emma said shyly. "I think he's awesome, too.

And I do understand why you're so protective of your brother. I know about rehab."

A muscle in Madeline's jaw quivered. She eyed the door. "Keep it down," she whispered. "He told you?"

"Yeah. He told me the other weekend, when I ran into him at the grocery store." This was one time Emma could be absolutely honest. "And I haven't told anyone else. I wouldn't do that to you guys."

Madeline let go of a breath. "Thanks." She untied her hair and let its dark layers spill over her shoulders. "I love my brother," she said softly, taking a strand of hair between her fingers and examining a split end. "I just want him to be okay."

"I know," Emma whispered. "He's getting better, Mads. You said yourself he's been clean since he came home."

"As far as we know." Madeline stared out the window. Then, abruptly, she whipped around and met Emma's gaze. "I know I've been kind of crazy about my brother. But you can't imagine what it's like here without him. When he was spending time with you—and now with Laurel—he's not *here* . . ." Her voice trailed off. Tears filled her eyes.

"I can't be in this house without my brother, Sutton," she finally said, shaking her head slowly. "He's the only one who protects me, the only one who loves me."

"Oh, Mads," I whispered, watching all of this, feeling so powerless.

Emma wrapped her arms around Madeline's shoulders. "I'm here for you," she whispered. She might not be able to put herself in Madeline's shoes exactly, but she'd had her fair share of family drama, too, and she knew what it was like to be scared.

I wrapped my arms around both of them, wishing desperately that I could make everything okay.

Hours later, Emma woke with a start, her throat burning. It was 3 A.M., which Becky used to call the witching hour. Becky had been a night owl, and without fail, Emma would hear her pacing their apartment at 3 A.M. on the dot.

A tear-shaped night-light on Madeline's wall cast an eerie blue glow across the floor. The house was silent except for Mr. Vega's snores, which were audible from down the hall. Emma wanted to close her eyes and fall back asleep, but it felt like her mouth had been stuffed with cotton.

She pushed back the covers as carefully and quietly as she could. Earlier, while they'd watched TV and gossiped, Mr. Vega had stuck his head in, looking enraged. "Where are your physics books?" he'd seethed. Madeline had jumped nearly a mile. "Um, we're taking a break," she'd said. After that, they'd turned the TV off and barely spoken. Emma hoped Madeline wouldn't have to pay for that when Emma left in the morning.

The hallway bathroom was right next to Mr. and Mrs. Vega's room, so Emma decided to head to the kitchen instead. The stairs creaked beneath her weight. She froze for a moment, sure Mr. Vega would come screaming for her. *Just keep going,* she told herself, staring straight ahead and creeping toward the kitchen. *You aren't doing anything wrong.*

At the end of the hall, a curved wooden vase held skinny brown branches blooming with yellow flowers. An antique silver platter sat on a coffee table in a small sitting room. Emma crossed a Navajo-style carpet and rounded the corner into the kitchen, which still smelled faintly of spices from dinner. Just as her bare feet hit the cold tile, she saw something and gasped. Thayer stood at the black granite island. He was staring at her.

Emma jumped back. "Oh!"

"What are *you* doing here?" Thayer whispered. He'd been in his room with the door shut tight when Emma had arrived earlier.

He was wearing navy boxers and no shirt, and even the darkness couldn't cloak his muscular shoulders and stomach. She averted her gaze fast. "Um, Mads and I are having a sleepover."

My pulse ratcheted up. What I wouldn't give for a few more minutes—*alone*—with Thayer Vega and those shoulders.

Thayer's golden brown eyes traveled over Emma's flimsy tank top. "That's cool."

As hard as it was to watch Thayer look at Emma like that, a part of me wanted my twin to be even closer. I wanted Thayer to pull Emma to his chest so I could remember what it felt like to have his arms around me.

Then he stepped toward Emma. "It's been a long time since you slept over," he said, his voice rough around the edges.

Emma swallowed. Thayer was standing so close, she could smell his deodorant and the mint of his toothpaste. He glanced at the clock on the oven. "Three A.M.," he said in a low voice. "That was our old meeting time, remember? Is that why you came?"

"I—" Emma said haltingly. She wanted to tell Thayer no, but something was stopping her. It was like he was a magnet, yanking her toward him. "I just needed a night away from my dad."

Suddenly, his arm was around her waist, and his lips were just inches away.

"Thayer," Emma said, turning her head.

"Sutton," Thayer breathed into her ear.

"I-I'm with Ethan now," Emma blurted. She stepped away from him. "I should go."

Thayer held up his hands. "So go."

Emma knew she should leave. She really did. But something kept her there, staring at him for a moment too long. His hazel eyes drew her in. She could practically taste how much he wanted her.

"I—" she whispered, but the rest of the sentence evaporated on her tongue.

Don't, I begged silently. *Please. Give me a few more seconds.* But then I felt the heartbreakingly familiar snap as she fled back upstairs to Madeline's room, dragging me behind her, away from the boy I still so desperately loved.

~ 26 ~

CALL THE DOCTOR

Thursday afternoon, Emma steered Sutton's car into a parking space in the visitor lot of the University of Arizona Hospital and Medical Center. Sweat instantly prickled her temple, but whether it was from the blazing sun overhead or the fact that she was about to break into Mr. Mercer's office, she wasn't quite sure.

A doctor dressed in sea-green scrubs emerged from the front door, talking on her cell phone and fidgeting with the stethoscope around her neck. As she passed Emma, she gave her a small smile. Emma ducked her head and didn't smile in return, feeling like a spy.

Could she really do this? Sneak into Mr. Mercer's office

and look through his stuff? Even though Emma and Ethan had agreed it was the best thing, she'd wrestled with the prospect. She might have shoplifted, participated in Lying Game pranks, and even ransacked Laurel's and Thayer's rooms all in the name of hunting down Sutton's killer, but something about going through Sutton's father's office felt way more dangerous. Maybe because it was a hospital, a place with tons of video cameras and security. It would be so easy for Mr. Mercer to find out what she had done.

Steeling herself, Emma swallowed hard and strode toward the elevator bank, pressing *3* with her index finger. That was where Mr. Mercer worked—she'd seen it on his business cards.

Orthopedics was to the right of the elevators, and Emma strolled there as casually as she could. The place looked like any other hospital she'd ever been in: greenish walls, tall windows, and linoleum floors. The eerie smell of antiseptic and sickness hung heavy in the air, and there were drawings on the walls done by patients from the children's wing, most of them colorful, oblong dragons or sad-eyed dogs.

I scanned the halls, too, waiting to find something familiar, some object that would spark my memory. Had my dad brought me here after he killed me? I couldn't help but picture him carrying my body through the corridors and down to the hospital's incinerator.

Emma turned a corner and entered the surgery waiting room. A receptionist in a feather headband regarded her warily from behind the front desk. "Excuse me, miss? Can I help you?"

Emma froze. The woman's eyes scanned her without a hint of recognition, which was probably a good thing. "Yes, actually, I'm here to see Dr. Mercer. I'm a patient of his." She tried to look distraught, like she had a serious problem that merited Mr. Mercer fitting her in at the end of the day.

The receptionist narrowed her eyes. "Dr. Mercer isn't in today. He's at a conference."

Shit. Emma realized she should have planned her cover better—of *course* the receptionist knew where Sutton's dad was. Suddenly, though, a small man in a hospital gown and with white bedhead hair wandered down the hall. Clutching a bag of potato chips, he peered around the room as though looking for someone.

"Grover?!" he called. "Grover, are you here?" Then, grumbling, he continued down the hall, sliding in his socked feet across the linoleum like he was ice-skating.

The receptionist stood and moved away from her post. "Mr. Hamilton!" she called. "Now how did you get all the way out here?" She rested her hand gently on his bare arm and led him through a bank of doors.

Emma seized the opportunity and took off down

another long hallway marked OFFICES. She eyed the room numbers hungrily. 311. 309. 307. *Bingo.*

Be unlocked. Please, be unlocked. Emma pushed the silver handle down and used her elbow to shove the door open and shut behind her in one fluid motion. She was in.

Mr. Mercer's office was a perfect square and smaller than she'd imagined. A single window looked out to a man-made pond and garden. Four framed diplomas—all of them from schools in California—hung on the white walls, and a calendar with a photo of Drake romping in snow at some rustic cabin hung next to the wood desk. A leather chair was pushed back, like Mr. Mercer had abruptly shoved away from his desk and bolted from the office.

Emma heard footsteps and instinctively threw herself against the door. *Do not come in!* Her heart thudded in her ears until the footsteps receded.

Then she looked at the desk itself. It had three drawers, plus a file cabinet. An appointment book sat atop a blotter, and a Mac laptop was positioned near the lamp. Slowly and carefully, she opened the top drawer, not quite sure what she was looking for. A bloody knife? A bra belonging to his paramour? A signed confession? But all the drawer contained was a prescription pad, a bunch of pens, and a pocket guide of medications and symptoms.

In the next drawer she found a mountain of paper clips,

yellow highlighters, and a solar calculator. Manila folders packed with medical records sat on top of notepads marked with pharmaceutical drug names. She yanked open the third drawer to find an opened box of ballpoint pens and a checkbook. She flipped to the back where the log was kept. *Score.* Mr. Mercer was one of those types who still balanced his checkbook by hand instead of online. She scanned his messy handwriting, which had documented checks for a gas bill, the mortgage, several hundred dollars to a Tucson catering company called Let's Bake Bread!, a Visa payment, Internet, and cable. Then there was a check for two hundred dollars paid to someone named Raven Jannings.

Emma didn't think much of it—she could be a massage therapist or one of those people who do deluxe men's shaves. But then she flipped the page to find another check, this time for five hundred dollars, made out to Raven again. And then another, and then another. They were always varying amounts, always round numbers, and always on a Monday.

Pulling Sutton's phone from her pocket, Emma googled Raven Jannings. But nothing came up besides Google's suggestion to redirect her search to Raven-Symoné.

The black phone on Mr. Mercer's desk rang, and Emma jumped. The caller ID flashed on the screen. *Super 8 Motel*, it said, showing a local Tucson number. Emma wrinkled her nose. What kind of surgery patient stayed in a seedy highway motel?

The call ended. Emma waited a moment, staring at the small triangle at the corner of Mr. Mercer's phone. She'd worked at the front desk of a Vegas motel once, and they'd had a phone just like this one—the triangle lit up green when a voicemail was left.

The phone rang again, and the same number appeared on the caller ID. Emma stared at the receiver. Something was telling her to pick it up.

Me, maybe? I was screaming it as loud as I could.

Cautiously, Emma lifted the phone. "Hello?" she answered, her voice unsteady.

Ragged breathing sounded on the other end.

"Hello?" Emma asked again. "Is anyone there?"

More breathing. "Uh, wrong number," a woman's voice said. She hung up fast.

Emma's heart pounded, a new idea taking form in her mind. Was that *her*? Mr. Mercer's mistress? And was her name Raven?

My mind swirled. Was my father seriously having an affair with someone named Raven? *Gross!* And did they rendezvous at a Super 8? Maybe he figured no one would run into him there—my mom clearly wouldn't be caught dead at a seedy motel. The whole thing made me feel like I was covered in ants.

Emma slammed the phone down just as the door handle to Mr. Mercer's office turned. *Shit.* She dropped beneath the desk, crouching into a tiny ball in the space where the chair normally went, and pulled the chair in close to mask her. *Please, please don't be him*, she thought frantically.

A female voice started to hum softly. Emma's fist slowly unclenched. A heavy stack of papers thudded on the desk above her head, followed by the sound of something being dropped into a tin box. Emma held her breath as the woman shuffled around the office, her footsteps muffled by the industrial carpeting.

When the door clicked closed again, Emma heaved a huge sigh and crawled out from beneath the desk on shaky legs. She shoved the checkbook back into the top drawer, then pushed the chair back a few feet, just as Mr. Mercer had left it. She was just out the door and around the corner when she heard a voice behind her.

"Dr. Mercer!"

Cautiously, Emma peeked back around the corner and saw a nurse in pink scrubs handing a file to a doctor just out of view. "Thanks very much," a familiar voice said. Emma's blood ran cold. It was *Mr. Mercer.* Why was he back so early from the conference?

She watched in horror as Mr. Mercer strolled to his office, files in hand, and shut the door behind him. Her heart was rocketing so fast she could barely breathe. She had *just been in there.* She had *just missed him.*

It was like divine intervention. I'd say I had something to do with it . . . only I didn't.

Emma bolted into an open elevator and pounded the button for the ground floor. As the doors clanked shut, she leaned against the back wall and tried to catch her breath. That was way too close a call.

Anger swelled within me as the elevator descended to the ground floor. Emma wasn't the only one making lists now: I'd started one called *Ways My Father Lies.* Dutiful husband? Caring father? Ha. I thought about the checks he'd written to Raven, whoever she was. The breathing on the other end, the seedy motel she was staying at. I thought about them meeting there, doing things I didn't dare consider.

And then, finally, I thought of my dad operating on his patients, his hands steady, meticulous, and precise. I could only imagine that they had been just as capable as they forced the light from my eyes, and the life from my body.

27

THIS MEANS WAR

When Emma pulled into the Mercers' driveway a half hour later, she was relieved that Mr. Mercer's SUV was nowhere in sight. She dreaded coming back, but she dreaded more what might happen if she didn't. She opened the front door and dumped Sutton's keys next to a stack of envelopes on the shiny black table in the foyer. Then she padded past the photographs that lined the hallway—Sutton and her father posed on vacations and family outings, always smiling. What a crock. Had he been thinking about Raven the whole time? And what had the checks he'd written her been for? Jewelry? Hotel rooms?

Or was it hush money to keep Raven quiet about what he'd done to me?

"Sutton?" Mrs. Mercer called from the kitchen. "Is that you?"

Emma stopped in the hall, trapped, as Mrs. Mercer emerged from around the corner. Emma ducked her head, feeling like everything she'd just found out was written all over her face.

"Hi, Mom," she said, her voice way higher than usual.

Mrs. Mercer's hair was piled on top of her head with bobby pins holding up the pieces near her ears. Other than a streak of blush on her high cheekbones, her face was free of makeup. She'd changed from work clothes into black jogging pants and a fitted zip-up sweatshirt with an Adidas logo on the chest. Tiny pearl studs still dotted her earlobes. *She's so beautiful*, Emma thought sadly. *And such a good mom. Why would anyone want to cheat on her?*

That was the question I kept asking myself, over and over.

"Are you okay, sweetie? Dad says you've been studying hard with the girls all week," Mrs. Mercer said, the smile melting from her face. "You look pale. The stomach bug didn't come back, did it?"

Emma's cheeks hurt from smiling so hard. "Oh, I'm fine. I just have this German test tomorrow. It's going to be *really* tough. And so much of my grade is riding on it." She tapped a fingernail against the railing. "I just need to lock myself in my room tonight and study. Do you mind if I eat upstairs, just this once?"

A smile spread across Mrs. Mercer's face. "Of course I don't mind. You know how proud your father and I are of your test scores so far this term."

Emma fiddled with the strap on her bag. The Mercers had made such a big deal about Emma's high test scores, lifting her grounding for shoplifting from Clique to attend Homecoming. Mr. Mercer, in fact, was the one who convinced Mrs. Mercer that their daughter should be rewarded for her hard work. But it had all been an act. Mr. Mercer knew the girl getting the test scores wasn't his daughter. He was probably just rewarding her for going along with being Sutton.

"I'll be in my room." Emma raced up the stairs two at a time. She shut Sutton's door behind her and collapsed onto the bed, listening to the front door open and slam, open and slam. First Laurel came in, then Mr. Mercer. High, happy voices sounded downstairs. To Emma, they were like nails on a chalkboard. All she could think about was that phone call from the roadside motel, the breathing on the other end.

When a loud knock sounded on Sutton's door, Emma shot up. Before she could say a word, the knob turned with a click, and the door creaked open.

"Sutton?"

Emma took in Mr. Mercer's face. His dark eyebrows lifted. Drake stood behind him, smelling of some kind of sickly sweet dog shampoo.

"You're back." Mr. Mercer held a plate of pasta slathered in tomato sauce. "I heard you were eating up here." He stood in the doorway. "Studying hard?"

Emma watched him. Surely he knew she wasn't really studying. But he was playing it cool, a smile on his face, a proud look in his eyes. "Uh-huh," she mumbled.

Mr. Mercer nodded. "It's amazing how you've improved since school started. A whole new Sutton."

Emma stared at Sutton's quilt, resisting the urge to be sick. *I'm a whole new Sutton because you killed the original*, she thought bitterly. *Are you happy that I'm doing exactly what you want? Are you glad you can continue your little affair in peace, you horrible murderer?*

All at once, she couldn't deal with him being in here another second. She jumped up from the bed, grabbed the plate and silverware, and turned her back. "Thanks, *Dad*," she said, spitting out the words. Then she kicked the door closed on him, and turned the lock with an audible click.

That's right, Sis, I thought. *Get him out of there.*

Once she was sure Mr. Mercer had returned downstairs, she grabbed Sutton's laptop and googled local Super 8 Motels. The second number listed looked familiar—she could have sworn it was the one that showed up on the caller ID in Mr. Mercer's office. Taking a deep breath, she dialed.

Someone answered on the third ring. "How may I help you?" It was a bored voice. The TV blared in the background.

Emma took a breath. "Can you connect me to Raven Jannings's room?" she asked in a barely audible whisper.

The concierge let out a yawn on the other end. "Sure thing," he said. "Please hold."

Emma's chest clenched. She'd guessed right. And suddenly, she knew she was right about everything else. The woman breathing on the phone call had to be the same woman Mr. Mercer was seeing. The same woman Thayer had caught him with on the night of Sutton's death. The same woman Grandma Mercer had called toxic.

There was a *click*, and then ringing. Emma's foot jiggled nervously. *Please, please, pick up.*

The call went to voicemail, a generic message that the guest staying in room 105 wasn't available.

"I have information for you about Ted Mercer," she said, before she could even consider her words. "I'm coming to your motel tomorrow night at nine P.M. sharp. Be there."

Then she hung up and stared at Sutton's iPhone. Was this really what she wanted? What if meeting with Raven was dangerous? Then again, who knew how long this woman would be at the motel? This might be her only chance.

I had questions, too. Had I met Raven that night in the canyon? Or had my dad just assumed I'd seen her and killed me anyway? Just what kind of deadly secrets was she keeping?

Be careful, Emma, I thought. *You could be walking into a trap.*

28

BREAKING AND ENTERING

Friday evening, the smell of crisp leaves greeted Emma's nose as she, Ethan, and Laurel walked up the steps to the school. A forgotten stainless steel Klean Kanteen glinted next to the gym door in the final rays of sunlight. It was 7 P.M., an hour after sports teams finished practice—and a half hour before the dance was scheduled to start. Laurel and Gabby had been right. The entire administration was away at a conference in Sedona, which meant they didn't have to worry about Principal Ambrose marching in and busting up the party.

A velvet rope had been set up at the back door of the gym. The bouncer Charlotte had hired stood there menacingly, looking the part with a headset in his ear and black sunglasses over his eyes. "Hey," Emma said cautiously, shooting him a smile, and he nodded in return. The gym door opened easily and without a click—Charlotte had made sure of that by taping down the lock with bright blue electrical tape.

Her eyes slowly adjusted to the darkness. Lili, Charlotte, and Madeline, all wearing the matching pink dresses they had selected at La Encantada the other day, were in the gym, hanging streamers, blowing up balloons, and setting up tables full of food. The place had already been transformed from a smelly exercise room into a chic club, with lots of curtains, tables, and even a cushy couch or two. The lights were turned down low, and the DJ was organizing his tables in the corner.

"About time!" Lili cried, clutching a butter-colored roll of streamers in one hand and a rusty pair of scissors in the other. Her hair was piled high on her head, and thick eyeliner rimmed her eyes.

"Hey, Mercer girls," Charlotte said from the top of a stepladder. Her red hair spilled down her shoulders, and her pink dress complemented her skin perfectly. She stuck a tack into a cardboard cutout of Jessica Rabbit. "And Ethan," she said, nodding in his direction. "Looking sharp."

"Thanks." Ethan smiled. He did look great. His dark

hair was combed off his face, and his blue button-down brought out his eyes.

"What's *that?*" Emma asked, watching the busty cartoon swing from her carrot-colored hair.

Charlotte shrugged. "I found it in my mom's closet and figured, why not?"

Madeline, whose hair was up in an artfully messy bun, snickered.

"So everything is set?" Emma asked, scanning the wooden tables lined against the bleachers.

"Yeah, is the footage okay?" Ethan said, checking out a silver laptop next to the food.

"It's great. And we're just about there, setup-wise." Madeline handed Emma a bunch of red cups in plastic sleeves. "You're on food duty. We need cups, plates, silverware, and everything unpacked from the coolers."

"Got it," Emma said, breaking the plastic wrap with her teeth. But as the girls turned away, the smile that had been pasted on her face faded. She knew she should be excited for the illicit dance—and in some ways, she was. But she was also terribly distracted by what she had to do later tonight.

She still couldn't believe she'd been ballsy enough to ask to meet with Raven. She'd called Ethan after to tell him her plan. He'd insisted she let him go with her—just in case. She'd added his worry about her safety to her

Top Ten Cutest Ethan Moments list, but it wasn't until now that she considered that he might be right. What if this just spelled disaster? What if Raven had contacted Sutton's dad already? What if Emma and Ethan showed up at the motel and found them both waiting for her?

Madeline's phone beeped, jarring Emma from her thoughts. "They're on the move?" she said into the receiver. "Perfect. We'll expect them in five."

She stuck the phone back into her clutch and looked at the others. "That was Gabby. She's in her car, following the Devious Four, who are *obviously* on their way to our party. We'd better mobilize. Char, is everything in place?"

"Yep," Charlotte said, giggling slightly.

Ethan moved to Emma's side. She narrowed her eyes and squeezed his hand. "What are you guys up to?"

Charlotte smiled slyly. "Oh, we thought we'd add something extra, along with the video projection on the wall. Just to remind them never to mess with us again."

Ethan gave Emma a skeptical look, and she pulled her bottom lip into her mouth. Just one more thing to add to her *Things I Hate About the Lying Game* list: *Taking everything a step too far.* "It's nothing dangerous, is it?" The last time the Lying Game had pulled a prank without her knowing, she'd ended up trapped in a rocky crevice in the desert.

Madeline snickered. "God, Sutton. Don't worry about it."

Before Emma could ask more, a bunch of kids streamed through the unlocked door. The girls had on party dresses, and the guys wore ties and khakis. Madeline dimmed the lights further, and the DJ started a loungey song to kick off the night.

Lili materialized at Emma's side again. "They're here!" she hissed. "The Devious Four are here!"

Emma peeked out the gym door. Sure enough, the bouncer had lowered the velvet rope and was talking heatedly to the four girls, who were dressed to the nines.

"What do you think it is?" Ethan asked out of the side of his mouth.

"I guess we'll see," Emma said nervously.

"But we were *invited*," Ariane, the girl with the dip-dyed hair, argued, tugging on the leather skirt of her dress.

The bouncer held up his clipboard. "Not according to this list, you aren't."

Lili nudged Emma. "I told him to give them a hard time. But now he's going to ask Coco to prove she's a Hollier student by going to her locker . . . which is right next to the gym." She grinned maniacally, then flagged down a girl Emma recognized from English carrying a video camera. "Sadie! I need you in the hallway! Something major is about to happen!"

Emma chewed on her lip as the bouncer lifted the velvet rope and let the Devious Four inside. He followed them to Coco's locker, and the girl with the video camera skulked behind them. Coco spun her combination, looking annoyed. Emma braced herself for what could be inside. What if it was something that really freaked them out—or worse?

I didn't like this either. I didn't want to be responsible for hurting anyone else.

The video camera blinked red, its lens focused on the girls. Just as the latch clicked open, there was a *whoosh-*ing sound. Suddenly, something spilled out of the cubby, gathering in a mound at each girl's feet. Emma squinted, taking a moment to realize what the white tube-shaped objects were. Tampons.

"Ew!" Ariane said, grabbing for the cottony tampons, which had all been unwrapped from their plastic shells. The other girls jumped away from the tampons, but they kept spilling from the depths of Coco's locker. Then, they looked up and realized they were on video camera. Their faces went red. Ariane put her hand on the lens, angry-celebrity style.

"Smile!" Charlotte trilled, leaning against the door-way. She gestured to a wall in the gym, where the girls' images were projected. "You're live!"

The Devious Four all turned in the direction she

was pointing, their mouths hanging open. And as they watched, the footage switched from the live feed of the tampons at their feet to the security feed Ethan had success- fully downloaded. A grainy image of four girls decorating the trees in the courtyard with bras and panties appeared on the wall, flip-book style. At first, it was hard to see who the vandals were, but then, one of the girls turned, stared straight at the camera, and gave it the finger. She had trademark two-tone hair and a bratty smirk.

Gotcha, I thought. My friends couldn't have pulled this off more perfectly.

"Ethan, it looks amazing," Emma breathed.

Ethan grinned. "I have to admit it's pretty fun to be on *this* side of the prank."

Everyone in the gym was watching. First there were whispers, and then they turned into stares and grumbles. "It was *them!*" plenty of people said. "Who *are* they?" someone else cursed. "Losers!" a voice called over the rest.

The Devious Four hung their heads. They stared at the members of the Lying Game, who had all gathered in the doorway to accept their victory. Emma stepped forward and plucked a tampon off of Ariane's shoulder, a smirk on her face.

"Now you know who bows down to whom," she said lightly, spinning on her heel.

Way to go, Sis. They totally deserved it.

★ ★ ★

An hour later, the party was in full swing. A rap beat pulsed through the huge speakers the DJ had positioned all around the bleachers. The disco ball spun, strings of lights flashed on and off, and bodies danced in a massive swarm under the basketball hoops. Sadie roamed with a handheld camera, and members of the yearbook staff patrolled with big SLR cameras, snapping photographs like they were the paparazzi. Hollier students had gone all out, as though this was a normal dance—some of the girls wore full-length dresses and most of the guys wore ties.

"Um, I thought we were keeping the guest list small," Emma said, scanning the packed room. At least a hundred kids were there.

The Twitter Twins looked at each other guiltily. "Well, people kept asking to come . . ."

Madeline blushed. "Yeah, I ended up inviting some people from the dance studio."

"Who cares?!" Charlotte shouted. "This party is awesome."

The song ended, and the DJ's voice boomed through the microphone. "This next one is dedicated to a certain group of girls—you know who you are. Thanks for throwing such an amazing party, ladies!" The opening beats to "Sexy and I Know It" swelled through the air. Everyone screamed and ran for the dance floor at once.

Lili barreled up to Emma, who was supervising the food table, and grabbed her arm excitedly.

"We so rock!" Lili shrieked.

Emma grinned in return. For the past hour, kids had come up to her, thanking her for throwing the party and complimenting her on the decorations and music. It was official: The girls of the Lying Game were back on top as the queens of Hollier.

If only *I* could share some of the glory. Nostalgia filled me as I watched my friends. I remembered exactly how a night like tonight felt: the sheer thrill of orchestrating a prank, the buzz I felt when I walked into a packed party and decided who was lucky enough to be on the receiving end of my attention, the whoosh of heat when I locked eyes with Thayer across a room.

But then Emma checked her phone, and her stomach tightened. It was almost eight thirty. She had to leave soon.

Suddenly, a warm hand circled the top of her arm. "Can I have this dance?" Ethan said in her ear. While Emma had been holding court, he'd been talking to some kids from their German class.

"Of course!" she breathed as Ethan pulled her close. His lake-blue eyes held hers. He leaned forward and brushed Emma's lips with a kiss.

"Awwww!" Lili swooned, snapping a Twitpic.

Emma grabbed his arm. "Let's go somewhere quiet," she whispered into his ear.

Ethan nodded, and they pushed through the crowd together. Students brave enough to talk to the girl they thought was Sutton Mercer congratulated her on an amazing party, and Emma flashed a confident smile. One girl dressed in head-to-toe purple asked to take a photo of "Hollier's Hottest Couple." Emma and Ethan paused for a moment, smiled, then moved on. Normally, Emma would have nudged Ethan and commented on how ironic it was that a foster kid and a loner were suddenly an It couple, but now wasn't the time.

As the opening notes to a Coldplay song blared, Emma pulled Ethan under the bleachers. "Okay. I admit it, I'm nervous about tonight," she said.

Ethan's eyes narrowed in concern. "You don't have to go, Emma. There's got to be another way."

"Maybe, but I don't know what it is, and I can't just continue on like this, not knowing." Emma twisted the silver bracelet on her wrist around and around. "Living in that house is making me crazy."

"But what if Raven is in on the murder? What then?" Ethan asked. "Maybe this *is* too dangerous."

Emma thought about this, staring at the students in the gym. Most of them were dancing or laughing by the snack table. "Maybe it is dangerous. But that's a chance

I have to take. Please back me up, Ethan. *Please*. I don't know what else to do."

Ethan still looked worried, but he pulled her into a hug. "I understand," he said. "I've got your back. I'll be there every step of the way."

Emma set her jaw. "Actually, I was thinking about that. If I bring you to the room, it could freak Raven out."

Ethan paused, running a hand through his hair. "Okay, what if I wait outside the room?"

I liked that plan. The last thing I needed was my sister dying and *both* of us being in the in-between, trying to figure out who killed us.

"Deal," Emma said.

"Please be careful, okay?" Ethan looked worried. "I don't know what I'd do if anything ever happened to you."

Unexpectedly, tears filled Emma's eyes. "I'll be okay."

"How can you know that?" Ethan pressed.

"I guess I can't," Emma said, fidgeting with Sutton's silver locket at her collarbone.

"I'll be right outside the room. And if you get a bad feeling, or if something doesn't seem right, promise me you'll get out of there."

Emma forced a smile. "Of course I will."

Ethan leaned forward and put his arms around her again.

"When this is all over, think of how much easier it will

be for us," Emma whispered in his ear. "I'll just be . . . me. And you'll just be you."

Ethan pulled her closer to him, but his gaze was elsewhere. A bunch of bulky figures stood in the doorway. "What the . . . ?"

Suddenly, the music screeched to a halt. There were confused murmurs. Emma and Ethan made their way out from under the bleachers just as Madeline's voice rang out. "Cops!"

"Everyone, freeze!" one of the figures called at the same time.

Pandemonium ensued. Students shoved toward the doors, nearly knocking Emma to the ground. Several police officers ran into the gym and grabbed students. Sirens whooped outside, and megaphones blared instructions to freeze and stay calm.

Emma grabbed Ethan's arm. "Come on!"

They cut into the mass of kids. Girls hobbled toward the door, unsteady in their heels. Guys took shortcuts over the bleachers, stumbling over the risers. A lacrosse player who'd had too much to drink bumped against Emma, breaking her grip with Ethan. He was drifting away from her, like a life raft cut from its ship.

"Ethan!" Emma called out.

Students elbowed between them. A cacophony of screams and cries echoed through the air. Someone caught

Emma's shoulder, and she turned to see Nisha's eyes flashing.

"Hurry!" Nisha called.

Emma turned back for Ethan, but he wasn't in the spot where she left him. "Ethan!" she cried out. "Ethan!" She checked her watch. It was 8:40. She had to get out of there. She couldn't miss her meeting with Raven.

Students poured into a hallway that led to the parking lot just as a police car screamed up to the entrance. Wheeling around, she sprinted in the opposite direction, down an unfamiliar passage. She kept looking over her shoulder, hoping Ethan would materialize, but he was gone. *Maybe he'll meet me outside*, she thought. *He knows where to find me.*

She continued down the hall, Sutton's sandals rubbing blisters on her feet. The hallway was dark, and she could barely see in front of her. She thought she could make out a door at the end of the hall, but what if it led nowhere?

Suddenly, there were footsteps behind her. "You!" a voice called.

Emma spun around, recognizing the voice instantly. *Quinlan.* Of course *he* would be the one to find her.

But she couldn't let him get her—and she couldn't let him figure out who she was. She sprinted faster, her lungs screaming.

"You there!" Quinlan's voice sounded even closer. "Stop!"

Emma's hands reached out and touched something hard just seconds before she crashed into it. She pulled away, seeing a bookshelf lined with old texts. She felt around for a door, but there was none. "Oh my God," she whispered. She'd hit a dead end.

Quinlan's walkie-talkie squawked. "I've got one," she heard him say.

Emma looked down, then up. Her heart lifted. A small window glowed a few inches above the shelf. Even better, it was slightly ajar. Her fingers grasped a middle row of the bookshelf, and she set her feet on the bottom row and started to climb. The structure swayed back and forth as she shimmied up the shelves.

"Stop!" Quinlan's shape was visible down the hall. He was running at a full sprint, his club raised above his head.

Emma pulled herself up to the top of the bookshelf and cranked the window as wide as she could. The space was just big enough for her to fit. She turned onto her stomach and stuck her legs through the window. Her fingertips caught the metal grooves of the window frame as she pushed herself through and dropped onto the ground. Her knees bent to absorb the impact, and her hands hit the grass hard. Then she took off running. She was *free*. She'd done it. And Quinlan didn't know who he'd almost caught.

But I felt less than thrilled for my sister. As I watched Emma bolt through the darkness, I wished she would have thrown herself in front of Quinlan and let him haul her downtown, even if it meant getting arrested. I realized, as I watched, that I didn't want her to go to that motel—especially alone.

Answers were waiting in that room, I just knew it. And with those answers, came danger.

29

MOTEL HELL

"You are two miles from your destination," the portable GPS's tinny voice rang out through the cabin of Sutton's car. Not that Emma needed directions now—she could see the Super 8's neon sign glowing in the distance. Her stomach was a ball of nerves as she pulled off Route 10. In 1.9 miles, she'd have her answer. Now 1.8 miles, 1.7 . . .

She took a left at the intersection. Barely any cars were out, the streets were deserted, and the fast food restaurants that dotted the two-lane road were eerily empty. Emma passed an Arby's, a McDonald's, and a tired-looking diner called The Horseshoe that had a couple of rusty pickups in the parking lot. As a light drizzle turned to rain, she

254

rolled the window farther down and let the pelting water spray across her forearms. The chill kept her present and focused. She had to keep her composure no matter what she found at the motel.

Emma turned onto a dark, slick road, and the Super 8 loomed into view. VACANCIES, a sign announced at the entrance. But the *V* and *C* had burned out, and the *N* had tipped over.

Emma pulled Sutton's car around the back and angled into a parking space. Only a lone red truck shared the lot. Was it Raven's? She squinted hard at the Arizona plates, the big tires, the naked-girl mud flaps. Would she really drive something like that? Then again, she knew nothing about the woman. She could be anyone, into anything.

Emma stepped out of the car and locked it behind her. Rain pounded the premises, and an earthy smell rose from the desert beyond. She wound around the front of the motel and followed signs for room 105. Most of the windows were curtained, but the few that were opened revealed neatly made beds and tired-looking wood bureaus. A wrapper for a Filet-O-Fish lay crumpled in the corner. A spiderweb glistened from the eaves. Her sandals rang out loudly on the pavement, so she angled up onto her toes, trying to soften her footsteps.

Finally, she approached room 105 and stopped, her heart thudding so fast she thought it might implode.

Yellow light streamed through a crack in the dingy pea-green curtains. Peeking through, she saw that a television was on.

Fear twined through me. Was this it? Was my sister going to figure out what happened? I knew exactly what Emma was hoping for: a confession and hard evidence about my murder. But how likely was that?

Emma moved to the door and knocked gently, wondering what the hell she was going to say when Raven answered the door. A long moment passed, but she heard no footsteps inside. She knocked harder. Still nothing. She pounded the door so hard that the latch caught and the door inched open with a long, loud *creeeeak*.

Emma froze. A bedside lamp was on. The bed was neatly made with a yellow-and-green-striped comforter and two thin pillows. There were no suitcases on the hassock or clothes hanging on the small metal garment rack. The TV flickered cheerfully, showing a sitcom so old Emma didn't even recognize it. But the room was empty.

Okay, so then leave, I thought nervously. *Get the hell out of there.*

Emma glanced behind her, then stepped inside. A faint smell of cigarettes and stale bread filled her nostrils. "Hello?" she called softly. "Is anyone here?"

Her whole body shaking with nerves, she moved past

the television to the bathroom door, which was closed. "Raven?" She pressed her ear against the door, straining to hear movement.

"Raven?" Emma pushed the door open. Tiny bottles of motel shampoo and conditioner lined the sink. An unused bar of soap sat on the ledge next to a disposable razor. She moved to the shower and, with a flash of trepidation, tore the curtain aside. Nothing. She opened the plywood cabinet beneath the sink, hoping to find some sort of makeup bag or personal item stored there, but other than a plunger and spare roll of toilet paper, it was empty.

She padded back to the bedroom and searched the closet. There were unused hangers and an iron. The dresser drawers were just as bare.

She's not here, Emma thought with disappointment. Running her fingers through her hair, she sat down on the bed, trying to get her bearings. Her gaze fixed on the cream phone on the nightstand. The message indicator light wasn't flashing. Did that mean Raven had gotten her message? Had she taken off to avoid learning the "information" she'd promised about Mr. Mercer?

There was a low rumble of a passing car outside, sending a shock of fear through Emma's system again. Pushing off the mattress, she tiptoed toward the door, pausing to shut off the TV as she passed. It was then that she noticed a matchbook sitting on top of the TV, its cover

SARA SHEPARD

flipped slightly open and several matches pulled away. THE
HORSESHOE, it said on the front. Scrawled in black pen on
the inside were two words. *Meet me.*

Emma's heart leapt. She reread the words, her mind
scattering in a million directions. Was this message from
Raven? Maybe she didn't think meeting in the motel was
safe. Maybe she worried about getting caught or maybe
there was someone—Mr. Mercer?—watching.

Stuffing the matchbook into her clutch, she tore from
the room and slammed the door behind her. She ran fast
down the sidewalk, eager to get to her car. The Horseshoe
diner was so close—she'd passed it on the way in. She'd be
there in no time.

She was halfway across the parking lot when the glowing beams of headlights shot to life. Emma halted and
shielded her eyes. Parked in one of the middle spaces was
an SUV that hadn't been there when she'd gone into the
room. As her eyes adjusted, a hard pit formed in her stomach.

It was Mr. Mercer.

30

DINER DASH

The car door jerked open before Emma could run. She backed up against the wall of the motel as Sutton's dad climbed from the SUV. His face was a twisted mask of frustration and fury. "What the hell do you think you're doing here?" he shouted.

Emma tried to scream, but nothing came out. Images of what Mr. Mercer could do to her flashed through her mind. "Leave me alone!" she said in a small, weak voice.

"Get in the car!" Mr. Mercer barked.

Emma inched along the side of a windowsill, feeling her way with damp fingers. Maybe she could slip into the shadows and then run. Go to The Horseshoe, talk to Raven, call the police . . .

"I *said*, get in the car!"

Emma turned on her heel and started to sprint. There was a slam behind her, and she heard footsteps. Emma's feet slapped the pavement hard, and when her left ankle turned, she winced but kept going. The footsteps were gaining on her, though. When she dared to glance over her shoulder, she could see Mr. Mercer just a few feet away.

Go! I screamed. *Run!*

Emma's throat burned as she gasped for air. Black shadows danced along the walls of the motel. She was so close to Sutton's car—only a few more yards before she could lock herself inside it. She rounded the corner to the back lot and raced across the final distance. Mercifully, she managed to get the door open and the key into the ignition before Sutton's father reached her. The sound of the motor revving filled her with relief.

She backed out from the parking spot and peeled toward the exit. In the rearview mirror, she saw Mr. Mercer drop his hands to his knees. He looked like he was heaving, having a hard time catching his breath. *Good*, Emma thought as she sped from the motel's parking lot.

She turned left onto the main road and crushed the accelerator to the floor. She pushed the car to its max and gripped the steering wheel. The diner loomed ahead, and she made the final turn and screeched into the parking lot. This place had to have the answers she needed. Raven had to be there. Because if not—what was her next move? She couldn't go back to the Mercers. That much she knew for sure.

Deal with all that later, I thought. *Just go.*

The diner was long and thin with a dull, gray exterior, hedges that needed trimming, and windows that showed patrons eating fried potatoes, slurping coffee, or perusing menus. Dim lights flickered over the doorway, and wilted cacti lined the sidewalk. Emma pulled around to the parking lot behind the diner—she didn't want Mr. Mercer to see Sutton's car from the road on his way home.

The rain had let up when she stepped out of the car, and she hurried toward the entrance. A tiny bell jingled on the door, and the smell of eggs and greasy bacon was overwhelming. A line of short-order cooks behind the counter flipped burgers, and waitresses flitted between booths with coffee pots and ordering pads.

"Can I help you?" A sleepy-eyed hostess with crimped hair leaned on the hostess stand. She looked Emma up and down curiously, surely wondering why a girl in an expensive pink party dress and smudged makeup was at a down-and-out diner on a Friday night.

"Um, I'm meeting someone," Emma mumbled. "I'll just seat myself."

The hostess shrugged. "Whatever."

Barely any of the booths were taken, and the ones that were had multiple occupants: three teenage girls, an elderly couple who held hands over the table, and two guys in bright red mesh trucker hats drinking coffee. No one looked remotely like a woman Mr. Mercer would have an affair with—and furthermore, no one was looking at her cagily, preparing for a confrontation.

Emma moved past the tables, her heart thudding fast. A door marked LADIES beckoned at the end of the aisle. Emma pushed through it, her nose wrinkling with the sharp smell of lemony air freshener. "Hello?" she called through the room, her voice echoing off the pink tiles. "Is anyone in here?"

She peeked under the stalls, looking for feet, but they were empty.

She turned to the sink and splashed water onto her face. Had Raven left the note for someone else? Had someone else written on the matchbook and given it to Raven? Had she hit a dead end again?

She peered at her reflection and saw both herself and her sister staring back at her. *I won't let you down, Sutton*, Emma said silently.

She exited the bathroom and stopped at the register. An overweight lady with thin blond hair was punching numbers into a calculator. "Can I help you?" she finally asked in a bored voice.

Emma straightened to full height. "My name is Sutton Mercer."

"Good for you," the woman said, unimpressed.

Emma wound a piece of hair around her finger, feeling like an idiot. "Um, I was supposed to meet Raven Jannings here. And it seems she's gone already. So I was just wondering if she'd left anything."

The woman's expression suddenly softened. "Raven?" She glanced up at an oversized clock that hung above the entrance to the kitchen. "You've just missed her."

Emma's throat went dry. "She *was* here?"

"Yes." The woman nodded. "And you were supposed to meet her?"

"That's right."

I waited, breathless.

The woman held Emma's gaze for a moment, as if deciding if she was telling the truth, then reached under a stack of twenties in the register and pulled out an envelope. "She left this for you."

Emma's stomach fluttered. "*Thank* you," she said, grabbing it from her. She looked around, feeling eyes on her back. The teenagers at the booth were staring at her. So was an old man at the counter. This place was entirely too public to examine whatever Raven had left. She had to go.

She shoved open the door and felt the humid, post-rain

air swallow her body. Once she was in Sutton's car again, she tore open the envelope, her fingers shaking. Inside was a note with a Polaroid photo pinned to the top. At first, when Emma looked at the face, she blinked hard, certain that something had misfired in her brain. The quality wasn't perfect, but Emma recognized the narrow face, the slanted nose, the high cheekbones, and the jet-black hair. She turned on the overhead light and stared harder, but the features were the same. It *couldn't* be.

I gawked, too, and my mind sparked and expanded. A new memory pieced together, and I found myself zooming back in time.

31

A FATEFUL GOODBYE

My father's SUV tears across the earth, kicking up rocks and roots and cactus spines. I trip over mini hills and stray plants, wheeling my way into the darkness. What if my father has completely snapped? Things have been so tense lately, but I never realized it could come to this.

The moon passes behind a cloud and my eyes start to play tricks on me. Gnarled branches twist into phantomlike shapes. I take a sharp right, and just when I think I'm going to escape him, my foot smashes against a rock and I go flying. I fling out my hands to break my fall. Blood pounds in my ears. I can feel my skin stinging from where I've cut myself and I know I'm bleeding. I bite my lip to keep from sobbing.

My father pulls the car up beside me. "Sutton!" he says from the open window. "Are you all right?"

My palms and knees are on fire as I push from the ground and try to steady myself. A bird squawks in the air above us. The only other sound I hear is the wind whistling over the dirt and between the cacti. I suddenly feel very exposed—and trapped.

"Why are you running from me?" my dad cries. His knuckles are white on the steering wheel. "And where is Thayer?"

I blink at him. You know where Thayer is, *I want to say. But the look on his face is surprisingly innocent and worried.*

I step back an inch or two, confused.

"Did Thayer leave you out here alone?" My father sounds shocked.

The more I look at him, the more confused I feel. Despite the layer of dust on his clothes and the worry lines on his forehead, he looks like my dad again, not some crazed maniac. And his confusion seems genuine. Is it possible it was someone else? But who would try to hurt Thayer?

"Um . . ." I don't know whether to tell my dad what happened. Suddenly I'm not even sure what did *happen.*

My dad sighs. "I'm not going to say it again. Get in the car, Sutton. It's dangerous out here at night. You could get hurt."

Exhaustion overcomes me, and I walk around the side of the car and let myself in. As we slowly drive back down the hill, I realize I wasn't far from the main road at all. I can see the neighborhood across the street from the canyon easily now. Ethan Landry sits on his front porch, fiddling with his telescope and probably hoping to catch a better view of the full moon. Science geeks are into that kind of thing. Next door all of the girls on the tennis team are on Nisha's lawn, secretly smoking cigarettes. I feel a pinch of guilt—I was supposed to be there tonight for our back-to-school team sleepover. Instead, I'd chosen Thayer. And look where that got him.

"What are you doing here?" I ask. "Why did you chase us?"

My dad looks frustrated. "I wanted to tell you the truth. Except you ran away before I had the chance."

"The truth about . . . what?"

"About the woman I was with," my dad says. His body looks stiff as he arches forward and grips the wheel.

I whirl around to face my father. My pulse ratchets up as I put the pieces together. This was why Thayer had dragged me away from the overlook and practically pushed me down the trail. My dad was with another woman up in Sabino Canyon. Someone who wasn't my mother.

"Another woman?" I squeak.

"I can explain, Sutton," my dad says. "It's not how it looks."

But I know exactly how it looks—and what it is. Sabino Canyon is the perfect place to carry on a secret affair: It's super-romantic and very private. That's why I'd brought Thayer here tonight. "You're cheating on Mom," I spit. "What more is there to explain? I don't need to know the gory details, like what kind of freaking lingerie your trashy mistress prefers." My fingers curl on the door handle.

My father's eyes open wide. "Sutton," he says, grabbing my hand. "It's not like that at all." His foot slams the gas pedal and he curves the SUV into an abrupt U-turn. We're heading back toward Sabino Canyon.

"Where are we going?" I shriek. The car plunges into a hole in the dirt and pops back up again, throwing me off balance. My elbow jams against the window. "Let me out!"

"Sutton, if you could just give me a second, I'll explain everything." He navigates the rocky road, his gaze boring through the windshield. My nerves flare as he guns the car into the Sabino parking lot and skids over the gravel. His foot lands on the brake and the car crunches to a stop. Then he glances around like he's looking for someone. Other than that same rusted-out brown car, the lot is empty.

"Dad?" I press. "What the hell is going on?"

"It's not what you think—I'm not having an affair." My dad shifts the car into park. "I know you've been curious about your biological mom for a while now. And I know the fact that your mom hasn't wanted to discuss it is why you've pulled away from us in the past year." He closes his eyes and takes a long breath. "That woman you saw me with tonight, her name is Raven, but she used to go by Becky. Sutton, she's . . . your mother."

I stare at him. The words take a few seconds to sink in. "What?" And then, "You're having an affair with my mother?"

"No!" Mr. Mercer shakes his head quickly. His light eyes

*hold my gaze. "She's your mother . . . and she's my daughter.
Which means you're my* granddaughter."

*I suddenly feel like my mind won't work. Like synapses are
firing in all the wrong directions. "What are you talking about?"
I whisper.*

*"Kristin and I had Becky when we were much younger," my
dad says slowly, his eyes searching my face as if gauging how much
I can handle. "And Becky was very young when she had you.
You were just a few weeks old when she left you with us." He
opens his palm and reaches a hand out to grab mine, but I ball my
fist against my side.*

"Your mom—your grandmother*—and I moved to Arizona
from California for a new start. Becky's been in town for a few
months now, and she and I have been talking in secret. I think
Grandma, your great-grandmother, has figured it out, but if your
mother ever found . . ." He shook his head. "Then, when we
saw you tonight, well, we panicked." His voice sounds hollow
and distant, like someone speaking from the far end of a hallway.
"But if you want to meet her, she's just up that trail there." He
gestures through the windshield to the dark path. "I told her to
wait, that I was going to try and catch up to you. We could go up
there together."*

He smiles at me kindly, hopefully. And that's when I lose it.

*"Are you kidding me? I'm not going anywhere with you!" I
snarl. "And I have no desire to meet the woman who pawned me
off without a second thought."*

He reaches for my hand, but I slam back against the car door.
"Don't you dare touch me!" I raise both hands. "Stay away!"

His eyes widen. "Sutton!"

But I flail like an animal. I feel like an animal, a tiger trapped in a cage. I shove open the car door, climb out, and stagger backward. "This is so fucked up!" I scream. The word hangs in the air, a taunt—I've never used it in front of my dad before.

But he barely flinches. Instead, a look of deep regret and disappointment passes across his features. "Okay, Sutton," he says quietly. "I'm sorry. I really hadn't planned for you to find out this way. Let's just go home."

"Go home? With you? Do you actually think you're blameless in all this?" I can barely stand still. "You wait till now to tell me you're my grandfather? You were keeping a massive secret from me for eighteen years! I've asked you and Mom a million times who my birth parents were, and you lied every time, saying you didn't know! Was actually being related to me, actually being my grandfather, so horrible that you had to pretend I was adopted?"

"Sutton," my dad sighs. "Please."

But I back away from the car, my heart racing hard. "I'm not coming home with you tonight. In fact, don't think I'm coming home for a while. And if you know what's good for you, you'll cover for me with Mom—or should I say Grandma?"

I turn around and start to sprint. I am on fire with fury. I can't get away fast enough.

"Sutton!" my dad calls, worry filling his voice. "Where are you going?"

"I have friends," I snap. "People who don't lie to me."

I reach into my pocket for my phone and clutch it hard as I continue to run. My arms pump as I cross the dirt. I can call Madeline. She's been calling me all night, anyway.

I'm halfway up an incline when my dad yells to me once more.

"Sutton, please!"

I turn to glare at him. "Don't you dare come looking for me."

"Sutton," he says softly, the word coming out like a whine. His shoulders slump with defeat. "I'm ready to talk whenever you are," he says sadly. "And, I know it's a lot to ask, but please don't say anything to your mom, okay? This would ruin her."

"Gladly!" I scream. "Because she's not my mom! And you're not my dad."

My father recoils as though I've slapped him. I've never seen him look so sad. I disappear over the ridge, then hear his car door slam and the engine start. As the car rolls over the crest and disappears down the highway, I hope to God I'll never see him again.

⤙ 32 ⤚

GRANDFATHER CLAUSE

With shaking fingers, Emma unclipped the picture of the mother she hadn't seen in thirteen years and looked at the note underneath it. Her eyes raced over the words, barely believing them.

I recognized your voice on the answering machine immedi-
ately. I wish things had gone differently that night in the
canyon, but there's nothing you can tell me about my dad,
your grandfather, that I don't already know. If you have
questions, ask him. He's a good man.

There's nothing I can give you besides this photo of me

from when I was your age, and a piece of advice. Living with your grandparents gives you every opportunity in the world. I never appreciated that myself, but it's not too late for you. Be smart. Seize those opportunities and don't make the same horrible, life-changing mistakes I did.

Raven Jannings (Becky Mercer)

Raven was . . . *Becky?* And Becky was the Mercers' . . . daughter? And Grandma Mercer was her and Sutton's *great*-grandmother?

Yes, I whispered. *Yes, it's all so fucked up, but it's true.*

"Oh my God," Emma whispered. *Becky.* She couldn't believe it. Her own mother was related to the Mercers. And she had been here just moments before. Like she had been throughout Emma's life, Becky was so close, and yet so far. A specter, a memory.

Emma looked at the letter once more. "That night in the canyon," was the exact same phrase Mr. Mercer had used when he'd cornered her in the school parking lot. Suddenly a crack opened in her mind and pieces started falling into place. Thayer had seen Mr. Mercer with a woman . . . Becky. But he hadn't been having an affair with her—he'd been meeting her because she was his *daughter.* And it sounded like Mr. Mercer and Becky had come clean to Sutton. Had she been so upset to learn the truth that she'd run off, only to die shortly thereafter? Either way, it seemed she'd been wildly wrong about Mr. Mercer. Becky had called him a good man. Maybe his discomfort with Emma, his warning to play along, had been because of what he'd told Sutton.

He didn't do it, I tried to tell her. *I ran away from him. I ran away from the man who could have taken me home safely.*

A small knock sounded on the Volvo's window and Emma jumped. Sutton's father loomed before her. His dark eyes blinked and his brow furrowed with a distinct combination of sadness, worry, and exhaustion.

Emma stuck the note in her clutch, then fumbled with the levers on the door. A clicking noise sounded as the window began to open. She was no longer afraid of him. She was just tired—and confused. "How did you know I'd be here?"

I studied the man I'd been raised to think of as my adoptive father, observing the contours of the face I knew so well. I wasn't sure how long it would take to adjust to the idea that he was my biological grandfather, but as I stared hard, I began to see similarities between the two of us—well, counting Emma, the *three* of us. We had the same sloping nose. The same pointed chin. The same long, thin hands. How could I not have noticed this before?

Mr. Mercer lowered his head and rested his hands against the door of the Volvo. "She . . . Becky . . . called me, saying you wanted to meet her at her motel. She wasn't in the room, but this is her favorite diner."

Emma nodded. "She left a matchbook in her room with a note that said 'meet me.'"

Mr. Mercer shook his head. "She always did love scavenger hunts," he said with a wistful smile.

Emma smiled, too. Becky used to make scavenger hunts for her around the courtyard of their apartment building, leaving a piece of birdseed on the table as a clue to look in the bird feeder in the corner, leaving a scrap of *TV Guide* in the bird feeder as a clue for Emma to look on top of the TV in the apartment, and so on.

"Was she in the diner?" Mr. Mercer asked, interrupting Emma's thoughts.

Emma shook her head slowly. "No. She just left a note. And a photo."

A gust of wind rustled his short hair, making it stand up straight. He glanced through the window of the diner before turning to look Emma in the eye. "Can I sit with you? Just for a minute?" he asked.

Emma nodded. She rolled up her window as Mr. Mercer crossed in front of the car and opened the passenger door.

Mr. Mercer let out a breath and stared at the glove compartment. His hands rested in his lap and he hung his head, making him look like a little boy. "I should have had a real conversation with you after that night," he said finally. "I shouldn't have let you run away. Especially after Thayer had left you there all alone." His eyes darkened at the mention of Thayer.

Emma nodded, saying nothing. His words confirmed what she'd suspected: that he'd explained the Becky situation the night Sutton died—and that Sutton had run off, angry and upset. And if Mr. Mercer thought Thayer had left her in the canyon, then it followed that he hadn't hit him with Sutton's car. It also actually explained why he hated Thayer so much: He thought Thayer had ditched his daughter in Sabino Canyon.

"But right after you ran off, I was called into surgery," Mr. Mercer continued. "I hated leaving you there, but you were just so angry. I thought it would be easier to talk once you had some space. When I got back from the hospital that night, I started to write you a letter. Maybe if I explained things clearly, you'd understand why I didn't tell you for so long." He turned to face Emma. "It wasn't because I was ashamed of you. It was because I wanted to protect you from your mother. I love you more than you can ever know. You are *my* daughter, and I've loved you ever since Becky left you at our house."

Emma tilted her head, taking in his words. "You wrote a letter?"

Mr. Mercer shifted in the seat. "I didn't finish it,

though. By the next day, you were acting like it had never happened, and I wasn't sure what to do. But I *can* finish it—if you want. Or, if you feel more ready now, we can just talk."

Emma's mind whirred. If he had been called into surgery, he had a solid, easily verifiable alibi. There was no way he could have been out killing Sutton if he was in the OR. More than that, she had no idea why he *would* kill Sutton. He was her grandfather. The secret he was trying to keep was for *her* and *Becky's* benefit, not his.

My relief at the knowledge that my father hadn't killed me felt like fresh rain on my skin—cleansing, revitalizing, purifying. My dad was my dad again, someone I could love, someone I could wholeheartedly miss. It felt like my broken heart was healed. And Emma was right: It *didn't* make sense that he would have killed me. I could tell in his face that he loved me more than words could say. I could also tell that this tension between us was killing him, that the only thing he wanted to do was end the stalemate and make things better.

But then I remembered the memory, and I felt the sharp sting of regret. The last words I said to the man I thought of as a father—my real *grand*father—had been full of hate. If only I could go back and change things. Change *everything*.

Mr. Mercer adjusted his legs in the footwell. "You

know, she really did care about you in her own flawed way," he went on. "When I first heard from her again a few months ago, I was so thrilled. Kristin had had enough of the lies, but I never had the heart to turn Becky away. Dads and daughters . . . you know." He ruffled her hair gently.

Emma nodded, wondering what it must have been like for them all those years ago when Becky showed up with a baby. She would've been right around Emma's age. She wondered why Becky hadn't told them about her, their other granddaughter—and why she'd only given up one of her daughters. Perhaps she thought she could be a good mom to just one girl. But, of course, by the time Emma was five, Becky had given up on motherhood entirely.

"I could never erase her completely," Mr. Mercer went on. "But she's troubled, Sutton. She always has been. I've been giving her money here and there, but it doesn't solve the problem. It only makes it worse."

A mist covered his eyes and he blinked, looking close to tears. "I always felt so guilty. Like it must have been something your mother and I did wrong as parents." His broad shoulders slumped as though the weight of his sadness was too much to bear. "The whole situation has felt . . . impossible." His voice sounded suddenly panicked. "I love Becky. But she's made our lives very painful at times. And the way she treated you . . ."

Fresh tears sprung to Emma's eyes. She knew full well how messed up Becky was—she'd lived with her for almost five years. And yet she still missed her, every day. She was her *mother* after all, and that was a hard bond to break.

Emma raised her eyes to Mr. Mercer, her grandfather, fingering the letter from Becky in her open purse. If she could only tell him the final piece in the puzzle: that he had another granddaughter, Sutton's twin. But until Sutton's murderer was found, she couldn't. She'd be the prime suspect, the poor girl who'd stolen her twin's life to get out of foster care. Once again, she was back to square one.

But not entirely. The moon emerged from a patch of clouds and hovered in the middle of the windshield. She stared up at the same sky she and her twin had shared for so many years without knowing it, the sky Emma had gazed up into and wished for a family. She had lost Sutton and Becky, but she had found her family—her *real* family. A grandmother and grandfather. A great-grandmother. And an *aunt* in Laurel.

She leaned toward her grandfather and wrapped her arms around his shoulders. He let out a long sigh against her, squeezing tight. The car made a metallic pinging noise beneath their shifting weight.

"Will you tell me a little about her?" Emma asked into Mr. Mercer's chest. "About my mom?" There was so much about Becky she didn't know, so many details she craved, so many questions that had plagued her for thirteen years. "Like what she was like as a kid?" Emma asked. "How I remind you of her?" Her voice was so choked with sobs she could barely speak.

As Mr. Mercer pulled her closer, Emma could feel tears on his cheeks, too. "Of course," he said, running his hands over Emma's hair. "I'll tell you anything you want to know."

33
SHE'S BACK

The following day, Emma sat at an outdoor café in a shop-ping complex a few blocks from the Mercers' house, Sutton's laptop beside her. Twitter was open, and she slowly scrolled through tweets hash-tagged #HOLLIERSECRETDANCE. If the tweets were any indication, the dance was a complete success—everyone was raving about the music, the food, the hookups, and even the narrow escape from the police. Only a few people had been caught that night. The cops had ended up letting everyone go, and so far no one had told that the Lying Game had organized it. Emma and her friends were safe for now.

I hoped they would stay that way.

"Sutton?" Mr. Mercer's voice jolted Emma. She glanced up from the computer and saw him walking toward her from the Home Depot across the parking lot, a new shovel in his hand.

"Hey, Dad," she said, relaxing her shoulders. She'd called the hospital last night and confirmed that he was in surgery the evening Sutton died. It felt good to not fear his presence but to welcome it with open arms.

Tell me about it.

Mr. Mercer stood next to the table. He passed a hand over his graying hair. "Your mom said you were here. I have to do some weeding, but I was thinking, if you weren't busy, maybe we could take a hike later. Explore a different canyon. One we haven't tried before."

Emma couldn't help the grin that spread across her face. That sounded like code for talking more about Becky. They'd had a long conversation last night, and Emma had learned so much about Becky. Like how she watched *Cinderella* five times in a row when she was young, loving how the fairy godmother made her into a princess. How she liked peach ice cream, Emma's favorite flavor, too. That she adored school until about eighth grade, when she got kind of wild, and that she ran away from home in high school . . . and came back pregnant.

But there were so many more questions to ask, a lot of things Emma hadn't dared to inquire about yet. Like why

Mr. Mercer's expression clouded over when Emma tried to talk to him about the trouble Becky used to get into. Or why Mrs. Mercer didn't want anything to do with her anymore. Becky was her *daughter*—could she really be that callous? Or had Becky done something so horrible to her that Mrs. Mercer simply couldn't forgive her?

"I'd like that," Emma answered. She was about to suggest a Catalina trail Madeline had told her about, when a blue BMW pulled off the main road into the lot. Emma turned to watch Thayer's car park in front of the café.

Mr. Mercer's eyes narrowed. When Thayer saw him, he blanched, and Emma thought he might back up and leave. But then he shifted into park and turned off the engine. The driver's door swung open, and he climbed out of the car and walked toward Emma.

Mr. Mercer stared at him. "I thought I told you to stay away from him, Sutton." He tightened his grip on the five-foot-long shovel. It was the kind of thing that would've freaked Emma out just a day ago, but now that she knew the truth, it struck her as kind of funny: her grandfather, clutching a shovel and yelling at some guy he thought was trouble.

Emma pressed her hand on his arm. "It's okay," she said gently. "I invited him. He's cool—I promise. And just so you know, he didn't leave me in the canyon that night. He got hurt and had to go to the hospital. I *made* him leave."

Mr. Mercer shot a suspicious look at Thayer. "Okay. But I'm keeping an eye on you, understand?" he said, pointing the shovel at him before heading to his SUV, which was parked a few stores over.

Thayer looked shaken as he sat down next to Emma. "I'm not sure this is a good idea. I've actually been thinking of going to the police about what happened to me in the canyon." He kept his eyes on a twenty-something hipster with a fedora entering the café, as if nervous to see Emma's reaction.

"That's why I asked you to meet," Emma said urgently. "My dad isn't the one who hit you that night. It was someone else."

Thayer's head snapped up and he gazed into her eyes. "Are you sure?"

"Positive. Actually, I found out something crazy." Emma took a long sip of her iced tea. "My dad is my biological *grand*father. The woman he was with that night? It was my birth mom. His *daughter.*"

Thayer's eyes widened. For a second he looked like he couldn't quite believe it. Or maybe he worried that it was yet another prank.

"I'm serious," Emma urged. "They were meeting and we surprised them."

Thayer looked astonished. "You mean your birth mother has been in town and has never tried to see you?"

Hurt tears stung Emma's eyes. She'd imagined Becky walking back into her life so many times, finding her and scooping her up in her arms and telling her everything was going to be okay. But then she thought of the note Becky had left at the diner. She wanted nothing to do with her children—she hadn't stayed at the diner. She had "nothing to give."

"She just left me and never came back," Emma blurted out, thinking of the horrible day when Becky abandoned her at a neighbor's house. "And she *still* doesn't want to see me." A tear spilled down her cheek.

Thayer leaned over and put his arms around her. "Oh, Sutton."

"It's okay," she said, swiping away the tears that wet her cheeks.

"Does Laurel know about all this?" he asked softly.

Emma shook her head. "No. And my mom doesn't know what happened either." Her stomach suddenly jumped. "You can't tell Laurel. You have to promise me."

"Sutton," he said in a low voice. "You know you can trust me." He stared hard at Emma. "But what does that mean? Who hit me with your car?"

"I don't know," Emma murmured. "Are you positive it was a guy you saw behind the wheel?"

Thayer squinted, thinking. "I guess I'm not really sure," he said slowly. "I just assumed it was your dad since he'd been running after us. It all happened so fast. I think the person had dark hair, but I never actually saw a face."

A shiver shot through Emma. Was it just a car thief . . . or someone connected to this case?

Just then a car backfired loudly, and Emma's head snapped up. A rusted, brown car rolled slowly into the complex. It kept starting and stopping in front of each store. Thayer frowned and hitched forward. "Is that person looking for something?"

Emma leaned forward, too, as the car made its way toward the café. Someone was staring over the dashboard at them. Her mouth was drawn tight, her eyes were wide, and there was an eerie expression her face. It was menacing and threatening, wild and angry. Then Emma took in the eyes, that familiar nose, and high cheekbones.

"Oh my God," Emma and I whispered in unison.

It was Becky.

34

MAMA DRAMA

Time stood still as Becky's car slowly rolled through the parking lot. I stared into those hollow eyes, into that pit of a mouth, trying to recognize something of me in her, but all I saw was an unhinged woman. Someone troubled. Someone who definitely had issues.

And major secrets.

Suddenly, as Becky hit the gas pedal so violently the tires made a shrill squeaking sound, something clicked in my mind. That memory I'd had of my grandmother and my dad talking, the one where I'd lurked at the top of the stairs, surfaced once more, and I remembered what they'd been saying. They'd been whispering, but I definitely heard Grandma say the words She's mentally disturbed *and* She's violent. *My father seemed frustrated, saying,* We have to help her. Before it's too late. *Had I crossed paths with her the night I died? Because if she was as mentally disturbed as they seemed to think, who knew what kind of reaction she would have had when she saw me.*

I groped for the rest of that memory from the night I died, anything past the moment I'd yelled at my father and then turned away in a rage. But it was just a huge, gaping hole. And yet I knew something was there. Something that would scare me to no end. Something that would break both Emma's and my hearts.

Because the only thing more devastating than my adoptive father killing me and threatening Emma was if our real mother had done it all.

~ ACKNOWLEDGMENTS ~

Many thanks to Lanie Davis—without all of your hard work, this book wouldn't be here! You are truly amazing. Also thanks to Sara Shandler, Josh Bank, Les Morgenstein, Kristin Marang, Kari Sutherland, and Farrin Jacobs— thanks for keeping the mystery juicy! And huge thanks to Katie Sise, who helped bring this book into the world.

Much love to my parents, who are so amazing and strong, and love to Ali, Caron, Colleen McGarry, Kristen and Julia Murdy, and Barb Lorence. Special love to Kristian, and a huge hug to Samantha Cairl. All of you are awesome! Kisses!

Read on for a preview of
THE LYING GAME
book five

CROSS MY
HEART,
HOPE TO
DIE

A FAMILIAR FACE

I watched the two teenagers sitting together outside the Coffee Cat Café on a sunny Saturday morning. They leaned toward each other, their voices low and almost intimate, their bodies close but not touching. Most people probably thought they were a couple—a really attractive couple. The boy had high cheekbones and a lean, athletic build. His blue-and-green striped polo shirt brought out the green flecks in his hazel eyes. He was movie-star hot. But maybe I was just biased: Thayer Vega *was* my boyfriend, after all.

Or at least he was before I died.

The girl next to him looked exactly like I did, back

when I had a body. Her bright blue eyes were lined with my velvety chocolate liner, and her light brown hair spilled down her back in thick waves just like mine used to. She was wearing a gray cashmere sweater and dark-wash skinny jeans from my closet. She answered to my name, and when a tear streaked down her cheek, my boyfriend leaned over to hug her. Instantly, I felt the ghost of my heart constrict.

I should have been used to this by now: living a bodiless existence as a dead girl, floating around like a plastic bag behind my long-lost twin, Emma, watching her inhabit my life, sleep in my bedroom, and talk to the boyfriend I'd never get to kiss again. The night Emma and I were supposed to meet for the first time, I never showed up—because I'd been murdered. My killer threatened Emma into taking my place, or else. She'd been living my life for months now, trying to solve the mystery of my death. But knowing all of that didn't make it any easier to watch moments like the one I was seeing now.

When Thayer had first returned to Tucson from rehab a few weeks ago, Emma had thought *he* might be my killer. But even though he was with me that night in Sabino Canyon, her investigation proved—to my great relief—that he definitely hadn't killed me. She had cleared my adoptive parents, too, even though they had been hiding a huge secret from me—that they were actually my *grandparents*. Our birth mother, Becky, was their troubled daughter. She had us when she was a teenager, leaving me with her parents and taking Emma with her when she left town, only to abandon her in foster care five years later.

I watched Thayer and Emma talk until a car backfired loudly. Emma's head snapped up, her gaze locking on a brown Buick idling in the parking lot in front of the café. The woman at the wheel had a wrecked look to her, her hair a wild black tangle, her cheeks sunken and pale. And yet I could sense that she'd once been pretty.

When I looked back at Emma, her hands were trembling. Her coffee cup tumbled to the patio tile, and the lid flew off, spilling lukewarm coffee all over her black flats. But she didn't even flinch.

"Oh my God," Emma whispered.

And just like that, I knew: It was Becky, our birth mother. I recognized her from Emma's memories, although she looked even more ragged than the last time my sister saw her, thirteen years ago. And yet she seemed familiar to *me*, too. I wondered if we'd ever met. So far, I had only been able to remember my life in disjointed flashes, usually preceded by a disconcerting tingling sensation. I felt tingly right then, but when I closed my eyes, I saw nothing. I had found out about Becky the night that I died. My father had met Becky in secret that same night—what if I had, too? I concentrated on the tingling feeling, willing myself to remember more of that night. But my mind was a blank and I was left with a feeling of dread and doom.

Just last night, my father had told Emma that Becky was troubled, possibly even dangerous. As I watched the car take off in a cloud of exhaust, I couldn't help but wonder: Was she disturbed enough to kill her own daughter?

I

DRIVE-BY MOM

Emma Paxton stared hard at the woman in the Buick. At first, all she saw was a haggard woman with a lined face, sunken cheeks, and cracked, thin lips. But then she realized that beneath her dull, spotted skin the woman had a familiar heart-shaped face. And if Emma squinted, she could picture the woman's brittle, frizzy hair a shiny, raven black again. And her eyes—those *eyes*. An electric jolt ran through her. *Our eyes are our best features, Emmy,* her mother always used to say, as they stood in front of the mirror in whatever run-down apartment they happened to be living in that month. *They're like two sapphires, worth more than any amount of money.*

She gasped. It was . . .

"Oh my God," she whispered.

"What did you say, Sutton?" Thayer Vega asked.

But Emma barely heard him. She hadn't seen her birth mother in thirteen years, ever since Becky abandoned her at a friend's house when she was five.

The woman looked up and her eyes—two blue sapphires—locked on Emma's. Her nostrils flared like a spooked horse's, then there was a gunshot-like bang and the car peeled away in a thick cloud of exhaust.

"No!" Emma cried out, leaping up. She clambered over the wrought-iron railing that surrounded the café's patio, scraping her shin in the process. Pain rocketed through her leg, but she didn't stop.

"Sutton! What's going on?" Thayer asked, hurrying after her.

She raced toward the Buick as it accelerated out of the parking lot and turned left into the Mercers' subdivision. Emma followed it across the street, barely noticing the traffic whizzing past her. Horns honked at her in anger, and someone even stuck his head out the window to yell, "What the *hell* are you doing?" Behind her, Emma heard Thayer's labored breathing and uneven footsteps as he did his best to keep up with her despite his injured leg.

The Buick turned down the Mercers' street and picked up speed. Emma forced herself forward at a faster clip, her lungs heaving in her chest. But the car pulled farther and farther away from her. Her eyes blurred with tears. She was about to lose Becky *again*.

Maybe that's a good thing, I thought, still shaken by my almost-memory—or, at least, my hunch. Whatever was going on, I had a feeling Becky didn't come to town for a happy family reunion.

Suddenly, the brakes squealed and the Buick screeched to a stop so quickly that the smell of burnt rubber permeated the air. A bunch of kids playing kickball in the street screamed, and a boy stood inches in front of the car, frozen in fear, a bright red ball in his arms.

"Hey!" Emma called out, sprinting for the car. She cut across the Donaldsons' lawn, hurdling their Kokopelli lawn ornament and narrowly dodging a staghorn cactus. "Hey!" she yelled again, plowing into the back of the car, bracing herself against the trunk to stop. She slapped her hand on the rear window. The exhaust steamed out hot against her knees.

"Wait!" she yelled. Her eyes met Becky's in the rear-view mirror. Her mother stared back at her. Her lips parted.

For a split second, it felt as if time stood still as Emma and her mother looked at each other in the mirror, cut off from the rest of the world. The boy ran off toward the sidewalk, clutching his kickball. Birds splashed in the Stotlers' rock fountain. The grumble of a lawn mower vibrated through the air. Was Becky hesitating because she thought Emma was Sutton? Or was she thinking of Emma, remembering all the good moments they'd shared? Sitting in bed, reading chapters from Harry Potter. Playing dress-up with the clothes Becky brought home from the dollar bin at the thrift store. Making a tent out of blankets during a thunderstorm. For five years, it had been just the two of them, mother and daughter against the world.

But then Becky broke her gaze. The engine snarled once more, and the Buick shot off in a billowing cloud of dust. Emma choked back a sob. She turned away—and stopped in her tracks. A police car had driven silently up behind her.

The driver rolled down the window, and Emma sucked in a breath. It was Officer Quinlan.

"Miss Mercer," Quinlan said acidly, his eyes hidden behind aviator sunglasses. "What's going on here?"

Emma turned as the Buick sputtered around the corner. For a fleeting second, she hoped that Becky had taken off because the cops had pulled up, not because she wanted to get away from her daughter. "Was that a friend of yours?" Quinlan asked, looking at the car, too.

"Um, no. I thought I recognized her, but I . . . didn't," Emma finished lamely, wishing it had been any other cop patrolling the street. Quinlan knew enough about her as it was—at least he thought he did. He had a file five inches thick on her twin, mostly about dangerous pranks she'd played with her clique called the Lying Game. Like the time Sutton had called the police to tell them she'd seen a lion prowling around the golf course, or the time she'd claimed to hear a baby crying in a Dumpster, or the time her car had "stalled" on the train tracks, only to miraculously spring back to life just in time to escape an oncoming train.

My friends had been particularly pissed at me for that one. They'd put together a revenge prank that was so dark, I hated to think about it even now. A video of it, which showed a faceless assailant strangling me, had been leaked on the Internet. And it was that video that had led Emma to me.

Quinlan squinted suspiciously. "Well, if you do know her, make sure she drives a little more carefully. She might hurt someone." He looked pointedly at the swarm of kids watching with interest from the sidewalk.

Irritation seized Emma. She crossed her arms over her chest. "Don't you have anything better to do?" she asked brazenly. Pushing the envelope was Sutton's M.O., and it felt liberating to channel her sister's attitude sometimes.

Thayer finally caught up to her, panting. "Afternoon, officer," he said carefully.

"Mr. Vega." Quinlan looked weary at the sight of

Thayer—he didn't trust him much more than he trusted Sutton. Thayer placed a hand protectively on Emma's arm.

I twitched. I knew Thayer was trying to be supportive, but I felt jealous all the same. I wasn't the kind of girl who shared, even with my own sister. Especially not my boyfriend.

Finally, Quinlan shook his head slowly. "I'll see you both around," he said, and drove away.

Thayer ran his hands through his hair. "Déjà vu. At least no one ran me down this time."

Emma laughed weakly. The night of her sister's murder, Sutton and Thayer had been together at Sabino Canyon. He'd snuck home from his rehab center in Seattle to visit Sutton, but what had started as a romantic moonlit walk had quickly gone sour. First, they'd seen Mr. Mercer talking to a woman who they'd assumed was his mistress. Then someone had stolen Sutton's car and rammed it right into them, shattering Thayer's leg. Sutton's sister, Laurel, had picked Thayer up and taken him to the hospital, leaving Sutton behind in the canyon. She had then met with Mr. Mercer, her adoptive father, who'd told her the truth about the woman he was with: Her name was Becky and she was Mr. Mercer's daughter—and Sutton's biological mother.

But as for what happened next, Emma wasn't sure. All she knew was that Sutton hadn't survived it. Emma had been piecing together that night in the canyon ever since she arrived in Tucson. Every clue brought her a little closer to the truth, and yet she still felt so far from solving the puzzle. She had figured out that Sutton, furious at Mr. Mercer's betrayal, had run back into the Canyon—but where did she go next? How did she die?

Emma looked down to see a ribbon of blood trickling into her sandal from the scrape on her leg.

"Here," Thayer said, following her gaze. He took a blue bandana from his pocket and knelt by her feet, carefully dabbing at the wound. "Don't worry, it's clean. I keep it on hand just so I can offer it to hot girls in distress," he added with a grin.

As the faded piece of cloth turned dark with my twin's blood, a memory flashed before me. I saw Thayer, his eyebrows furrowed, handing me that same bandana to wipe the tears from my eyes. I couldn't remember what I'd been crying about, but I remembered hiding my face in the fabric's soft folds, breathing in the warm sweet scent of Thayer's body that lingered on it.

"Who did you say that was?" Thayer asked, tying the bandana snugly around Emma's ankle to cover the wound.

Emma scrambled for an explanation, for yet another lie. But then she looked at the boy who'd loved her sister, his hazel eyes soft and concerned, and all that came out was the truth: "My birth mom."

Thayer blinked hard. "Seriously?"

"Seriously."

"How did you know it was her? I thought you'd never met."

"She left me a picture," Emma said, thinking of the note Becky had left in the Horseshoe Diner.

For a few horrible days, Emma had thought that Mr. Mercer killed Sutton, in order to keep her from revealing his affair. Knowing that Sutton had seen Mr. Mercer with a woman in the canyon, Emma had searched his office and discovered he was secretly paying a woman named Raven. She'd arranged to meet with Raven at her hotel, but the mysterious woman had sent her on a scavenger hunt that ended with a note at a diner. Raven had left behind a letter and a photo of herself—only, it had been Becky's face staring back. Raven/Becky had vanished, but Mr. Mercer had explained everything.

It was actually why Emma had asked Thayer to meet her for coffee. She'd wanted to tell him that Mr. Mercer hadn't been the one who'd run Thayer down in Sabino Canyon the night I'd died—and that the woman Thayer had seen Mr. Mercer with was actually her biological mother.

"It was her, Thayer. I know it was," Emma protested.

"I believe you," he said in a low voice.

Behind them a garage door rattled open, and they

stepped aside so that a freshly waxed Lexus could back out past them onto the street. They stood in silence for a moment, saying nothing.

"Are you going to be okay?" Thayer asked finally.

Emma felt her jaw tremble. "She looked . . . sick, didn't she?"

"She'd have to be sick not to want to talk to you." Thayer reached out and squeezed her arm, then pulled away cautiously, as though afraid he'd been too intimate. He nodded awkwardly back in the direction of the café. "I should probably get home. But Sutton—" He hesitated again. "If you want to talk about any of this, I'm here for you. You know that, right?"

Emma nodded, still lost in her thoughts. He was three blocks away before she realized that she still had his bandana knotted around her ankle.

I watched him go. Maybe he and Emma were right. Maybe the reason that Becky was acting strange was that she was ill. But I couldn't shake the feeling that I'd encountered her face before—while I was alive, before I became Emma's silent shadow.

I wondered if it had been the last face I'd ever seen.

Photo by Austin Hodges

SARA SHEPARD is the author of the #1 *New York Times* bestselling series Pretty Little Liars. She graduated from New York University and has an MFA in Creative Writing from Brooklyn College. Sara has lived in New York, Philadelphia, Pittsburgh, and Arizona, where the Lying Game series is set.

FOLLOW SARA SHEPARD ON

For exclusive information
on your favorite authors and artists,
visit www.authortracker.com.

PRETTY GIRLS DON'T PLAY BY THE RULES...
THEY MAKE THEM.

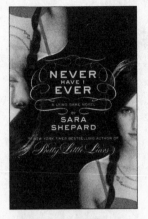
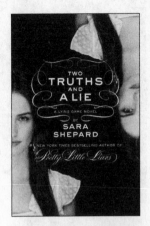

DON'T MISS SARA SHEPARD'S
KILLER SERIES THE LYING GAME—AND CHECK
OUT THE ORIGINAL DIGITAL NOVELLAS
THE FIRST LIE AND *TRUE LIES* ONLINE.

MY LIFE BEFORE I DIED, INCLUDING WHO murdered me, was a blank. My twin sister, Emma, had cleared my best friends, Charlotte, Madeline, and Gabby and Lili, as suspects. But the alibi she'd been counting on to clear my adoptive little sister, Laurel, suddenly wasn't so airtight. Laurel had a motive, after all. We shared a secret crush—and I was the one who got Thayer in the end.

Emma's keeping a close eye on Laurel, but if she's not careful, she'll end up just like me.

BOOKS BY SARA SHEPARD